CHALLENGING THE ALPHA

CORPORATE SHIFTERS

LILLY RAYMAN

LEILANI INDIE PUBLISHING

LEILANI INDIE PUBLISHING

Welcome to the Corporate Shifter world.
Nobody can run from their past...
Not even shifters.

This series is a collection of books sharing the same theme: corporate shifters.
In each story you will find a shifter who left their pack to join the corporate world, only to return and question if they made the right decision at all.

You can read these books in any order.
Return to Blackcreek by Quell T. Fox
Bear With Me by TJ Bell
Challenging the Alpha by Lilly Rayman
Claiming Emma by Leeah Taylor
For the Good of the Clan by Lucille Yates
Unexpected Mate by Morgan Meyer

To Rebecca, for her unwavering support and her dedication to helping polish my words and make them perfect.

❧ ☙

To Carole, and her enthusiasm for my work, and willingness to check for typos and stray commas before I upload.

❧ ☙

Most importantly, my husband and children for supporting me during the long hours that I spend talking with my characters and extracting their story — especially when the characters want to take a detour from the agreed-upon route.

CHAPTER ONE

CORD BUFFETT —
CALIFORNIA

Dispassionately, Cord looked at the escort slumbering face down on the bed. She had been exactly as he had requested. Tall, slender with toned curves in all the right places, auburn hair, and a flawless, alabaster complexion, requiring no makeup — as he had stipulated.

His gaze swept across the shadow of fingerprints marring the bare skin of her hips. Swallowing the lump in his throat, he shoved his toe into his Italian leather loafer a little more forcefully than he intended, wincing when the heel folded under his foot. Muttering under his breath, he pulled the leather back into shape and slipped his foot in with less vigour.

The woman slept on while he flicked out his jacket and shrugged it on over his half-buttoned shirt. More bruising was appearing on her thighs. Gritting his teeth, he extracted the billfold from his inside pocket and took out five hundred-dollar bills. The fee he paid her agency didn't cover the rough treatment she had received at the hands of his inner animal. It wasn't her fault, she just didn't 'do it' for him and his beast had come to the forefront of his mind to finish the job.

Padding out of the bedroom into the main room of the hotel suite, Cord looked for the woman's purse. It was where she had left it, on the wet bar in the corner. He opened the small black clutch enough to slide the crisp notes inside, then squeezed the clasp closed with a quiet click.

Not looking back, he left the suite and headed to the elevator in the small lobby. Hitting the call button, Cord tried not to look too hard at his reflection in the polished surface of the elevator doors. His eyes, such a dark brown they were almost black, looked dead to him in the artificial light.

Lip curling, he looked away from his distorted image. By night, his inner bear came into ascendency, taking control from him. It lit his eyes with a brightness that captivated most, if not all, of the women he met after dark. When the sun rose, however, Cord was left to his own thoughts, the bear slumbering deep within his subconscious, uncaring of the self-loathing and hatred that burned in Cord's chest.

The elevator doors opened with an almost inaudible hiss. He stepped in, one hand lifting the cuff of his expensive suit to check the time on the Omega around his wrist. 4.18 am. Too early to call his half-brother. Releasing the sleeve, he shoved his hand into his pocket, fingers fiddling with the few coins he kept in reach to distract himself when his mind raced, the other hand punched the button to the ground floor.

His skin always crawled when the moon was full. It was why he had given in to his bear and called for the girl he had just walked away from. Something about the phases of the moon encouraged shifters to want to mate when the lunar cycle was at its peak. He couldn't satisfy the itch with his own hand, yet he struggled to find the right woman, the one who tempted the man as much as she sated the beast. With the moon beginning to wane, he should be able to suppress his inner urges for a while, especially given he had slaked his thirst, rather savagely, last night.

Cord rocked back on his heels when the elevator bounced to a stop, the doors slid open revealing the muted lighting of the foyer.

The night manager stood when Cord strode towards the desk. "Mr Buffett, is everything okay, sir?"

"Yes, thank you, Rebekah. I'd like to settle my account. My guest, however, is still in the room. If she hasn't checked out by 6 am, could you please organise to have a continental breakfast sent up? Include it on my bill now, please."

"Of course, Mr Buffett. I will page the valet to bring your car round now, sir, before I finalise your account."

Cord nodded and, rested his arm against the polished marble of the reception desk to watch the light rain falling in a gentle curtain of shimmering light through the glass doors of the hotel.

The discreet clearing of a throat behind him, wrested Cord out of his moment of quiet solitude. He turned to see a bright white sheet of paper on the counter.

"Cash or card, sir?"

Cord glanced at the total, handed over several crisp notes, and scrawled his name across the bottom in a harsh slash of black ink. He looked at Rebekah briefly. "Keep the change."

She lowered her head a fraction, the hint of a smile curving her lips, as she retrieved the signed invoice. "Very kind of you, sir."

With a tap of his knuckle against the marble, Cord gave a sharp nod and stepped away. Headlights cut through the darkness of the early morning, washing out the softer glow of the outdoor lighting that lined the path from the hotel doors to the curb side.

The automatic doors whooshed open at Cord's approach. He was hit by a blast of frigid air carrying the sharp scent of rain and wet concrete. It cleansed his palette after being inside the air-conditioned hotel for several long hours.

The matte-black Lincoln Continental drew up in front of Cord, and the understated growl of the engine idling, while the valet climbed out of the car, was music to his ears.

The valet gave a low whistle, as he rounded the front of the vehicle. "Nice ride, man."

One corner of Cord's mouth lifted at the compliment, his eyes never straying from the sleek lines of the bodywork. He handed over a hundred-dollar bill to the valet and walked to the driver's side door.

The valet gave a big wave as Cord slid onto the buttery-soft leather seat, his hand searching for the lever to adjust the seat. He shoved it until he could fit his long legs in comfortably. Buckled up, he put the car in gear, switched on the wipers, and drove away from the hotel. At this hour of the morning, traffic was light, and he was able to merge onto the road quickly, heading for route 210 out of Downtown LA towards his home in the San Gabriel Mountains. The quiet road and lack of traffic to navigate, meant Cord could let his mind wander.

⟫⟫⟫ ⟪⟪⟪

Fire followed by ice exploded across his jaw. Cord shook his head, and blinked, trying to clear the stars distorting his vision after the upper cut had powered through his defences.

He bounced backwards, the canvas flexing under his weight. He hugged his elbows in tighter, and raised his fists a little higher.

The canvas swayed and lurched, as his sparring partner danced around him, fists jabbing so quickly, even with Cord's shifter increased ability, he strained to focus on the big man opposite him.

Left, left, right.

Right, left, right, left, left.

Eyes narrowed; Cord watched for the single tell. The one move that gave away a feint from a solid punch.

His opponent transferred his weight to the ball of his left foot.

Cord swung to one side, dodging the sharp right hook that skimmed past his ear. With the advantage in sight, Cord double tapped his fists against his partner's ribs, reining in most of his strength.

Vince folded. His defence dropped as, instinctively; he wrapped an arm around to cradle the sting in his weak spot.

A quick left cuff from Cord, and his opponent hit the canvas.

Flat on his back, Vince shook his head and spat out his mouth guard. "No fair, man. You know those ribs are still healing."

With a shrug, Cord mumbled around his own mouth guard. "I pulled my punches."

"Yeah, that's what stings more. You barely touched me and still got the drop on me."

Cord undid the Velcro on his sparring gloves. He shook the first one off, catching it between his knees which allowed him to pull the other one off with ease. Sticking the Velcro together on the two gloves, Cord removed his mouth guard and ran his tongue over his teeth to regain normal sensation.

"You're the one always telling me to fight through the pain and push to the next level," Cord said, offering his hand down to hoist his friend up.

Vince snorted. "That's what all good trainers are supposed to say. Don't mean we should do it ourselves. I'm old and burnt out, remember, that's why I teach, 'coz I can't do it anymore."

It was Cord's turn to snort. "Burnt out, my ass. If you hadn't won the local competition bout a couple of months ago, I'd have been inclined to believe you."

Water bottle poised halfway to his mouth; Vince glared at Cord. "That's what burnt me out!"

"Give it a couple of months and you'll—" Cord stopped speaking when he spotted the gym door open. His half-brother, Benny, poked his head into the room.

"You got a minute, bro?"

Cord nodded and turned back to his friend. "Sorry, Vince. I'll be back in a minute."

Leaning over the ropes, Vince waved him away. "Don't mind this old fart, Cord. I'll just get back my wind in peace while you go talk shop. We'll grab that coffee when you're finished."

Cord climbed out of the ring, jumping lightly onto the sprung floor of his home gym. He put his mouth guard and gloves on the bench near the boxing ring and grabbed a towel. He slung it over his shoulders, wiped his face and walked towards his brother.

"What?" he hissed following Benny out of the gym into the hallway.

Benny screwed up his face and raked a hand through his hair. "We may have a problem."

"What?"

"In Oregon. I've been able to get the contracts lined up for most of the businesses, all the small ones that is. The mayor is facilitating the lion's share of the sales, which surprised me, and she wants to finalise them with Buffett Property Group in person. That's not the issue. I haven't been able to contact the owner of one of the biggest businesses in the area."

Cord rubbed at the sore spot on his jaw. He wasn't used to Benny coming to him with a problem. Cord gave him a direction, and his half-brother went for it, not coming back until he had completed his challenge. "Which business? If you mean the bar—"

"It's not the bar. It's—"

"BearHeart."

Benny winced. "Yeah. I think it's going to need a personal touch."

"Then get there yesterday," growled Cord.

Benny straightened his spine. "Well, you can be the one to tell Elena. You already said I could have the next six months off. We get married in two days...two days, Cord, and then we are cruising around the world. You even suggested it...remember?"

Cord pinched the bridge of his nose and spun away from his brother. "Yeah. You need to go do that. I'll go to Oregon myself."

"*You*?"

"You think I can't handle it?" Cord, his head turned towards his brother.

Hands thrown up in surrender, Benny sucked in a deep breath. "Oh, I *know* you can handle it. You just hate being in the field. You'd rather hide in the office while I do the face-to-face PR work. Why not send Jeff, he's been a great wing man."

Cord shook his head. "I would only trust you for this job. I'll handle it."

Benny propped himself against the wall. "I still don't understand your game plan, bro. Why are you so hell-bent on acquiring complete businesses, not just property, and in another state altogether for that matter? This is not your usual MO."

Cord faced his brother. "It's...just...trust me on this, okay?"

Benny grinned. "I do, but once I walk into that church on Saturday...I'm not giving you, or your hare-brained schemes any more thought!"

Laughter rumbled out of Cord, "What? You won't be thinking of me on your wedding night? I bet Elena will be."

"You take that back," snapped Benny. He straightened to his full height of six foot and still craned his neck to stare at his brother.

Cord grinned, his fist bumping off his brother's jaw. "You know I hope you'll both be very happy together."

The two men hugged it out, each clapping the other on the back.

Benny caught Cord's forearm, stopping him from returning to the gym. "I love you, bro."

"Me too." Cord dipped his head, and Benny headed for the stairs leading out of his brother's basement, while Cord opened the gym door.

"Hey, Vince, you ready for that coffee now?"

CHAPTER TWO

STEVIE RAHAL — OREGON

Overhead the skyline screeched, the cables twanged as the carriage whirled along the cables. Wood creaked and metal screamed, the lassoes strained, and the first of three logs to be flown to the yard for processing was snagged on a gnarly stump. Stevie grimaced, as the logs splintered with the repeated collision against the still standing wood, until, with a shower of chips the timber broke free, dragging further up the hill.

The carriage rolled forward then lurched back. The grind of metal and wood reverberated through the corridor of trees when the second log got hung up against the same stump.

Vexed, Stevie whirled around to survey the other choker setters in the crew. "Are you assholes too fricken lazy to buck out that damn stump, or are you happy wasting our time and the boss's, watching wood bang all day?"

The resounding twang of metal behind Stevie heralded the release of the second log, the whirl of the carriage hopeful, until wood crashed together once more. The last of the logs that had been lassoed to the choke cable followed suit and caught on the stump.

Lip curling back, exposing bright white teeth with a low rumbling growl, Stevie attempted to stalk up the steep edge of the corridor. Instead, she bounced from one felled tree to the next until she reached the battered work truck parked on the edge of the field of fallen timber. Dropping the tailgate, Stevie pushed her hands against the metal, hauled her five-foot nothing frame over the edge, and crawled towards the bank of chainsaws laid out in the back of the truck.

Grumbling under her breath, she clasped the bar of her own saw, dragged the machine towards her, and shuffled backwards until her steel-capped toes slipped off the edge of the tailgate. She landed on her feet, bending her knees to reduce the impact of her jump.

The whistle tooted three times, a signal to the yarder that the final log was free and the operator could, at last, haul the load up to the landing. Stevie watched the three logs swing high, twisting and turning together, as the carriage flew them towards the processor for bucking.

Removing the cover and tossing it into the truck, Stevie hefted the bulky chainsaw onto her shoulder. With the weight adjusted, she found her balance to trek back down the corridor, the stump in her sights.

She reached the rest of the choker setting team, gathered in a loose circle sharing chewing tobacco in the short time they had available to them. Bobo, the hooker, jerked his head back, his scratched hard hat wobbled but never fell off. "Yo, Stevie? You plan on bucking that stump?"

"No," sarcasm dripping like venom, she snapped back, "I'm gonna drive Miss Daisy to church."

She stomped past. The other guys jeered and laughed, making Bobo spit out his plug of chew with distaste.

Ignoring the boys behind her, Stevie came to the stump. She dropped the chainsaw from her shoulder, seizing the handle in one smooth motion. A petite woman, despite the additional strength of being a leopard shifter, Stevie had developed her own way of pull starting the heavy Husqvarna. With the rope in her left hand, she lowered her right, gravity taking the weight of the machine towards the ground. The engine roared to life with only half the effort pulling alone required.

Choke off again, Stevie revved the engine until bar oil filled the guide and spattered the ground. She found her footing, flipped the chainsaw around and started cutting the stump just above the earth. Halfway through, the stump started to pinch closed, forcing Stevie to yank out the machine. It let go faster than she anticipated, and her eyes widened at the racing chain zooming straight at her face.

She locked her arms outward and stepped back. The whizzing saw swung her away from the stump, yet she managed to maintain her grip. With feline grace, she moved around to the other side of what was left of the Douglas Fir. The chainsaw sunk into the wood, cutting through the stump with ease. This time, the withdrawal of the blade was more controlled.

Stevie killed the engine, ensuring the chain had stopped spinning around the bar before she hoisted it onto her shoulder. The heat of the worked blade seeped through the flannel of her plaid shirt, spreading to the tight muscles of her biceps, providing discreet relief while she slogged back up the slope.

Overhead the carriage rumbled back towards the tail end of the corridor, the loose choke cables swaying in the air. Bobo tooted the whistle, communicating with the yarder to lower the chokes.

The boys jumped into action, each of them grabbing a choke and riding it down towards the butt of their target log. Stevie paused to watch. Like a well-oiled machine the rest of the setters lassoed three more trees and jumped clear.

"Clear."

"Right-o."

"Clear."

The whistle tooted three times. The carriage engaged, whirling along the cable. Wood and steel groaned while the chokes tightened and hauled the logs up the corridor towards the landing. Stevie nodded when the first of the three smashed through the stump. The block of wood rolled away, tumbling free of the three logs now soaring almost hundred feet in the air towards the processor.

Heat enveloped her, caressed her limbs, and sank into tired, sore muscles while she floated in the dense layer of bubbles, in her oversized bath. Despite the battering her body took working as a logger, Stevie didn't mind the lifestyle. She liked being a cutter, felling trees and clearing a road for the skyline, but she preferred choke setting. She enjoyed the camaraderie of the crew, and the varying degrees of banter between the men. Stevie was friends with all of them, well...all except Robert 'Bobo' Benson. The boys of BearHeart Logging had no objections to a woman joining the crew. They didn't even seem to mind that she was a leopard shifter and not a bear. She pulled her weight and got on with the job.

Bobo had been friendly at first, flirted and carried on like a strutting peacock, until she set him straight. He had missed her gentle cues indicating she wasn't interested, so she had no choice but to be more direct. She hadn't intended the rest of the crew to witness her put down, but it was what it was. He would just have to get over it. Of course, he was now smarting and gave her shit any chance he could.

The only young female in the Arabian-Panthera leap, Stevie knew how to give as good as she got. There was no point being shy and retiring growing up with boisterous cats. Of course, as her brothers grew up, the leap dwindled. The males had dispersed across the shifter territories of Africa, Arabia and even travelling as far as America.

Stevie and her American mother had headed for the United States. Initially staying together, but soon Stevie left her mother — who wanted to settle on the East coast — and followed her instincts, which led her to the Pacific Northwest. She wound up in the territory of the Torben tribe, finding herself being entertained in Muldoon's bar by a cocky, young bear.

Despite an inherent wariness of bears, Stevie felt comfortable in the company of Rygard Jones, owner of BearHeart Logging and son of the Torben alpha. It hadn't taken much convincing on his part for her to accept a job with the bear crew and learn all she could about logging, and of that, there was still much to master.

The water around her body started to cool, interrupting her internal musings. The languor of her body didn't encourage movement, so she slipped her foot out of the water, one eye cracked to guide her big toe with its red-painted nail to the hot tap and nudge it on. Heat poured over her feet, seeping into the bath water, curling around her body. She lowered her foot and swilled the water around letting the warmth envelop her. Her toe coaxed the tap closed and she wallowed, her nose all that was left above the bubbly surface.

Bath time was her indulgence in life, and the very reason she had rented this particular house. Diminutive in stature, with nothing but lean lines, the giant bathtub dwarfed her and, when combined with the honeysuckle and jasmine fragrance of her favourite bubbles, created the sensation of floating in a hot lagoon.

A pair of hands landed on her shoulders. She was pushed down until her back scraped the hard bottom of the tub. Air rushed out of her lungs, bubbles poured from her nose, her chest constricted, and she fought not to suck in water. Her hands scratched and beat against the sinewy forearms attached to the hands holding her under.

As swiftly as she was submerged, she was hauled out. Gooseflesh prickled against her skin; the cooler air rushed around her naked, wet body.

Stevie gasped, and her body contorted, struggling against her assailant, her scream cut off when an aggressive mouth claimed hers.

Sawdust and sweat flooded her nose. Whisky and mint filled her mouth. Familiarity crashed over her and, for a moment, went limp.

She bit his tongue and rammed her knee between his legs.

His grip slackened so fast, she dropped like a felled Douglas Fir and, losing her footing, jarred her hip on the edge of the bath. Water and bubbles sloshed over her, spilling onto the tiled floor, soaking the shirtless man huddled on the ground.

"You bastard, Rygard," she spat, endeavouring to stand up in the slippery bath. She reached for a big, fluffy, towel and wrapped it around her body, then used his leg as a step when she climbed out of the bath.

"Babe," he croaked.

Stevie left the bathroom door open and, storming into her bedroom, wrenched open the top drawer of her dresser. She spotted him in the mirror, hunched over, large hands cupping his crotch, pain etched across his face.

"Don't expect any sympathy, Ry. What do you think you're playing at? Sneaking in and frightening me like that?"

She found her favourite hooded kaftan and shrugged into it, cursing when a finger caught on a hook of loose jewelled trim. Pulling her hand back into the sleeve, Stevie made a fist then slid her hand through with more care.

A pale faced Rygard lowered his lanky frame onto the bed.

"Don't get comfortable there," she snapped. "I'm going to get a beer."

He got to his feet with a groan, "What the fuck you drinking this time?"

She stifled a laugh. She had been trying so many different craft beers lately, Rygard had complained she was turning the staple drink of any decent logger into a 'fru-fru' experience.

"I found the perfect brand for you." Halfway down the stairs, she glanced over her shoulder.

Rygard ducked his head under the low ceiling beam, the colour returning to his face. "Dare I ask?"

She shrugged and bounced off the bottom step. Her feet sunk into the thick Persian rug which ran the length of the hall from front door to kitchen. She switched on the light and, with a light step, crossed the tiled floor to the refrigerator. Choosing two black and orange cans, she handed one to the man hovering behind her then popped the top on her own.

Rygard raised one brow and he read the label. "Arrogant Bastard Ale?"

Stevie hid her smirk behind the can, swallowing a large gulp of the strong brew.

Indignantly, he opened his can, drinking half the contents before he backed her up to the kitchen cabinets, towering head and shoulders over her. One hand around her rib cage, the other clutched the beer. "Is that really what you think of me, Stevie?"

Taking another mouthful of her beer, Stevie canted her head, eyeing the defined planes of his chest and, skipping past the cleft in his chin, focused on his mouth. "If the shoe fi—"

His mouth captured her words, cutting her off, he kissed her.

Stevie allowed him to draw her flush to his body, the cold press of the can caught between them did little to cool the heat racing across her skin.

His teeth nipped at the fullness of her lower lip, releasing it at the point of pain. "I think you need punishing for your sass, babe."

She laughed and shoved him off.

He relented, stepping away from the pressure of her hand against his sternum.

She danced towards the breakfast table, drank another slug of ale and dropped the can onto the Formica surface. "You think you can tame me, Paddington Bear?"

Rygard gnashed his teeth. "Don't call me that."

Her eyes rolled and she pivoted on her heel. "Either bitch at me, or come fuck me, Ry, but you and I both know you're not alpha enough to stop me from calling you whatever I want."

He downed dregs of his beer, crushed the can in his beefy hand, and stomped upstairs in her wake. Her attitude was the very reason he preferred logging to women. The trees didn't talk back and, as long as he put his cuts in the right place, they fell where he told them to. If it wasn't for the full moon, he would have marched out of her house already. Too bad he was as horny as a bitch in heat, and she was easier to get along with than the she-bears in town.

CHAPTER THREE

CORD BUFFETT — CALIFORNIA — ALMOST A YEAR PREVIOUSLY

The bottle of Macallan was almost empty. The level of ruby-hued single malt was visible below the blue label, and the gold lettering mocked Cord while he drowned his grief. His younger half-brother, Benny, snored from somewhere behind him. Their father, Abe, his eyes, red-rimmed with tears and Scotch, had gone to bed an hour ago. It had been two years to the day since Cord's mother had died.

Two years of going through the motions of eat, sleep, work, or any combination of the three with a liberal amount of drinking thrown in along the way.

Tonight, they had drunk more than normal, reminiscing together, all their favourite memories of Lizzie Buffett, wife of Abe, mother to Cord and Benny.

The bottle appeared to move when Cord reached for it. Grimacing, he reached again. The smooth glass slid under his fingertips before he closed his hands around the neck and lifted it in a salute to his mother's photograph. It hung in pride of place on the rough-hewn wood mantel morticed into the river stone chimney, which doubled as the back wall of the large open-plan living space of Cord's San Gabriel Mountain home.

He downed the remnants of the Scotch and twisted to stare through the expanse of glass that, during the day, boasted a magnificent view of the Angeles National Forest. There was a hot tub in the corner of the yard, illuminated by underwater lights. A multitude of fairy lights twinkled around the gazebo — which although hopelessly overgrown with honeysuckle, provided a modicum of privacy — casting a gentle glow over the rambling garden, fading into the encroaching forest.

A shadow moved across the corner of the yard. Something too big and lumbering to be a coyote. Cord frowned. California black bears lived in the National Forest and surrounding areas, but, in his Kodiak bear form, he had laid down his own territory markers along the boundary of his land. Being territorial creatures, the wild animals shouldn't cross his land. A shifter may be bold enough to cross a territory marker, yet there were no shifter lands nearby.

Placing the empty Scotch bottle on the bar behind him, he toed off his shoes and tugged his shirt from his slacks. He walked towards the sliding door in the corner of the glass wall, dropping his shirt on the back of the sofa. Benny was face-down on the wide cushions, mouth open, snoring into the slate-grey leather. Benny was human, like their father, Abe. They knew the truth of Cord's nature but were unsettled by his bear.

Cord had been conceived before his mother, Lizzie, had married Abraham Buffett. Cord's genetic father had been a bear shifter, a man who had seduced his mother and led her to believe she was his fated mate. Apparently, the man's sheer animal magnetism had been enough to cloud her judgement. The same way it was for most humans because, despite being aware that shifters existed, they remained an unknown quantity.

Lizzie had recognised the man for what he was, but was ignorant of their lore, not understanding whether he spoke the truth or not when he called her his heart and declared her his true mate. She had slept with him, dizzied by his words, seduced by his touch. Lizzie believed she had fallen in love at first sight.

Only it hadn't been true.

Another woman had woken Lizzie, swooping into her cabin in the backwater town of Pineville, Oregon, alerting her to an imminent danger. The stranger had warned Lizzie, she would be taken deep into the forest of shifter lands and hunted; she was about to be sacrificed to the harvest moon.

Lizzie had packed up and left, not even saying goodbye to her great aunt and her mate, a bear shifter. She returned to UCLA to complete her Architectural Studies and her internship at Buffett Property Group. Abraham Buffett had shown an interest in Lizzie prior to her ill-fated break, and when Lizzie found out she was pregnant after her experience in Pineville, it was Abe who had found her in a quiet corner of the office, distraught. She told him everything, from being swept off her feet to being scared out of town.

Although close to twenty years her senior, Abe, had offered to marry Lizzie, happy to raise the child as his own. Feeling alone and afraid, she had accepted. For nearly twenty-six years, they had enjoyed a blissful marriage, raising two sons, until a hit and run had robbed the Buffett men of the woman they loved the most in the world.

Removing his slacks, Cord stepped outside into the cool, mountain air. Closing the door silently, he moved away from his lodge, his nostrils twitching as he tried to pin down the scent of the intruder. Despite being raised by human parents, he was comfortable enough with his bear to shift in the privacy of his own home, hidden deep off the beaten track of the San Gabriel Mountains, nestled against the edge of the Angeles National Forest.

He allowed the shift to race through him now, tingling across his skin. His body enlarged, his face contorted, and fur erupted. Upper lip raised, Cord let out a short, sharp huff and, clacking his teeth together, dropped onto all four paws to pad across the extensive lawn. The hum of the hot tub motor was overly loud in his sensitive ears, forcing Cord to hasten his step. He made his way through the natural arch of the cottonwood into the forest beyond.

There was another bear in the area. The stench of an intruder in his territory assaulted Cord's olfactory senses. He swung his massive head left and right, scenting the air, searching for the interloper.

There. Movement to his right. A stronger odour captured his attention, and he raced across the leaf litter.

The clouds shifted, and a weak beam sliced through the trees from the last quarter of moon hanging in the star-studded sky. Light glinted off the thick strands of white, lacing the dark fur of a smaller, black bear, who was sitting on his rear, back legs stretched out in front of him, front paws hanging loosely in his lap.

Cord bounded towards the other animal, challenging him with the threat of teeth and claw.

The older male turned his head aside, and his shoulders drooped, in tacit submission to the larger, younger Kodiak.

Cord paced around the hapless creature, inhaling the male's scent. Standing at full height, he towered over the black bear, then shifted into his human form.

"Shift," his command crackled through the air with the intensity of his anger.

The air shimmered around the seated bear. His fur vanished to reveal the wrinkled skin of an older man. He dared lift his head, rheumy eyes looking straight at Cord. "Alpha."

Cord's eyes narrowed at the acknowledgement. Recognition teased at the periphery of his consciousness. He knew this shifter. *But how?*

∾≫≫≫ ≪≪≪∾

Cord paced up and down his office. The buzz of alcohol had burned away with his shift but, as much as he wanted another drink, he wouldn't while this stranger was in his home. Halting momentarily, Cord glared at the other bear shifter.

"Tell me again. Why did you call me alpha?"

The other male tilted his head a fraction. "Because you are."

"I've never lived in a pack or tribe, never met another shifter."

"Lizzie said you would be tough to handle." The older shifter shook his head ruefully.

In four strides Cord was leaning over his desk, a glower marring his face. "What did you say?"

The cloudy eyes glinted. "Your mother, Cord. She said you would be tough to handle."

Cord ground his teeth, his words little more than a hiss. "My mother is dead."

"I know. I was at her funeral. Two years ago, in Glendale."

Recognition crashed to forefront of Cord's mind. An image of the man before him, shaking his hand, a gleam in his eye, as he had assessed Cord. He had been accompanied by a petite woman whose auburn hair was streaked with grey with a smile which reminded Cord of his mother. "You were with a woman."

The older male nodded. "My mate, Matilda."

Cord straightened and stepped back. "Flynn Muldoon?" an eyebrow arched in question.

"Aye." Muldoon nodded. "Everyone just calls me Muldoon though. Mattie is...was your mother's great aunt. It hit her hard, Mattie that is, when your mother disappeared in the middle of the night all those years ago. We heard from family that she was back at school. Were told when she got married and had her babies. But we never heard from her directly. Mattie loved your mother so much, it hurt to be cut out from her life."

With a snort, Cord slumped onto his chair. "Can you blame her?"

Muldoon looked baffled. "What?"

"With the harvest moon the next day she had to get away, and why would she say anything to either of you. You let that bastard take advantage of her, groom her for the ritual."

"Lad, I've no idea what you are talking about. What ritual?"

Cord's chair creaked as he shuffled restlessly. "You going to deny the harvest hunt?"

Muldoon pulled a face. "In all my years." He scrubbed a hand over his brow. "The Torben tribe have never held a harvest hunt, whatever that might be, and I've never heard of any other shifter tribe or pack doing anything of the sort. Where the hell did Lizzie get that idea?"

"She told me she'd been woken in the middle of the night and damn near dragged out of her bed by a terrified woman determined to save her from the depravities of the tribe and their alpha."

"*Depravities?*" Muldoon's brows knitted in bafflement. "*What* woman?"

Cord shook his head. "Mama never named her. Only told us a red headed woman had burst in, terrified, blabbering some horrific story about being taken into the forest by the alpha to be hunted and raped by the males of the tribe."

Muldoon's lip curled into a snarl. "Magda." He shoved back his chair and stomped across the room, hands clenched. His skin rippled, as he fought to control his inner beast.

Dread settled like ice in Cord's stomach. "Who?"

"Magda. The conniving little witch, she sank her claws deep into the alpha. The elders and I hoped he would grow tired of her, send her on her way. If she was a true mate, he would have claimed her immediately. I couldn't keep myself away from Matilda when I met her. I claimed her almost immediately." The old bear's knuckles cracked, then he took a seat on the couch tucked against one wall. "When Ryan first met Lizzie, we were certain they were true mates. Hopeful that the alpha would see sense and get rid of that clingy bitch of a human, Magda. We hoped he'd claim Lizzie, be everything the tribe needed him to be."

Cord stood and dragged his chair closer to the couch. "What are you saying, old man?" He sat down again.

"She lied," Muldoon roared. He lurched forward to grab Cord's hand. "That conniving little witch lied to our Lizzie. Magda must have seen them together, recognised the bond, Ryan couldn't see after she had manipulated him for months. I don't know how she did it, but she had him twisted around her little finger."

Cord yanked his hand out from the punishing grip of his great-great-uncle. "You're not making any sense."

"Don't you see?"

Muldoon's wild expression made Cord question the former's sanity. "See what?"

"You're the alpha's son and heir. Lizzie was always meant to be with Ryan. Magda tampered with the natural order of things. It's why the tribe is failing, why the alpha has gone mad. It's why you need to come back with me. Save the Torben tribe before another tribe works out how weak we are becoming."

Shaking his head, Cord stood. He needed space. Needed to think, and he couldn't do it listening to the ravings of a lunatic bear. He strode to the window. His breath condensed on the cold glass as he leaned against the pane.

Muldoon followed Cord, prodding the younger bear's taut shoulder. "I don't know what that woman did, but she lied to

Lizzie. Frightened her off, made sure she'd never come back. She made the alpha claim *her* as his mate, instead of your mother, his true mate. You know Ryan Jones is your father."

Cord whirled around, bellowing "Ryan Jones is *not* my father. You'd do well to remember that."

Muldoon retorted. "How else would you be a bear? Certainly not from that soulless human who dared to raise you."

"How dare you insult my pa? He's a better man than any god-forsaken shifter could ever be."

Head canted, his neck exposed, Muldoon apologised. "I'm sorry. I didn't mean to be disrespectful, alpha..."

"I'm not alpha—"

Muldoon ignored Cord's rejection of the title. "...I have a fondness for humans. My Matilda was a human. I'm not racist, I only meant you must have a shifter as your fathe...your genetic sire otherwise you would not be able to shift." He braved looking Cord in the eye. "I implore you, come to Pineville. You must help the Torben tribe get rid of Magda. She has buried her hooks so deeply into the alpha he doesn't know up from down anymore. Since your mother died ... well he never shifts anymore, let alone governs the tribe. The other elders and I do our best, but Magda rules the roost, giddy from her perceived dominance as the alpha's mate, running the show while Ryan trundles about the forest as a bear."

Cord opened his mouth to speak.

He was interrupted by Muldoon. "*You* are our rightful alpha, regardless of what you might think. Our tribe needs you." He stepped back, palms raised in surrender. "There. I've said all I came to say. I can do no more."

Cord watched the old man shuffle towards the door. Something niggled at his mind. "Wait."

The other male stopped but did not turn.

"You claim my mother told you I would be tough to handle, but you said you haven't seen or spoken to her since she left Pineville twenty-eight years ago."

A brief hesitation, then Muldoon faced Cord. "She wrote a letter. A letter she had arranged to be sent after her death. It didn't say much, but informed Mattie and I that her first born son was a bear shifter, and that he would need our guidance. She requested you be given time to grieve before we approached you." He inhaled a long steadying breath. "I never expected to find the pack's hope in our little Lizzie. Never expected parentage could be called into question. The letters we received from your grandmother led us to believe Abe had sired you."

"I'm not your hope," whispered Cord.

"We shall see." The cryptic words floated across the room, as the old bear left the study through the French doors, melting into the shadows of the unlit lodge.

CHAPTER FOUR

STEVIE RAHAL — OREGON

The truck bounced through another pothole on the rough track, jolting Stevie until her teeth rattled. She hated the rutted road up to the landing. Even the vibrations generated by almost eighteen pounds of roaring chainsaw several hours a day was less painful than the ninety-minute journey along this dirt track. Driving to and from work was one thing. Repeating it because Rygard wanted her to 'nip' the mechanic back to town was another kettle of fish.

Her shoulders ached, and her jaw throbbed. She was ready to tear into Rygard, and she would, but not in front of the crew. He would know she was pissed with him. Had already guessed if he was half smart.

The tall swathe of Douglas firs ended, the side of the road falling away down the steep hill. The barren landscape, a rugged scar left by the timber harvesting company. The grey-brown sweep of stumps and scattered branches jarred Stevie. It would be a couple of months before the planters came in, picking through the sticks and replacing the harvested wood with specially-ordered saplings.

The timber industry was only sustainable if it remained renewable. There would be nothing left for future generations if they didn't replace the thousands of trees felled each year. Knowing that in another sixty years the trees would be tall and thick once more, didn't make the sight of a recently hewn corridor any easier to handle.

Sunlight glinted in the distance. Blinded, Stevie shielded her eyes. "What the...?"

She slowed the truck to a crawl, frowning when she recognised the source of the glare. "Stupid yuppies," she muttered, hitting the brakes. The vehicle stopped behind a fancy, low-slung, sports car. The immaculate shine of the paintwork was sullied by the layer of road dust which had settled on the body.

Unclipping her seat belt, Stevie opened the door, stood on the running board of the truck; eyes fixed on the back of the driver's head. "Looks like you took a wrong turn, hey pal?"

The driver who had been perched on the front of the car, a cloud of smoke drifting above his head, stood. Stevie's eyes dilated, miles of arms and legs encased in an immaculately tailored slate-grey suit came into full view. Her mouth watered a little, as she drank in the vision.

He looked as though he had stepped out of a centrefold for Boardroom Weekly — if that was even a thing. If it wasn't, given the wet dream of a man in front of her, it damn well ought to be. His chest filled the double-breasted jacket, the expanse of snowy white shirt broken by the splash of colour from the half-undone blood-red tie. The top two buttons of the shirt were open, granting Stevie an opportunity to rake her gaze over the tanned skin of a muscular neck. A hint of black stubble, along with the thick cigar hanging from his lips disrupted her view of a strong jawline.

Her eyes reached the dark slash of his scowling brows, shadowing what would be considered a handsome face by most women. The well-proportioned set of his eyes to the Roman nose, and full lips. The negativity in his expression ended her fantasy. She disliked smokers, and brooding men. They made for unpredictable moods and tiptoeing around.

"No." His voice rumbled, deep and gravelly to the point she could almost feel it thrumming against her clit.

Stevie blinked, shaking off her body's unwanted reaction to the man. "Excuse me?"

He pulled the cigar from his mouth and walked towards her on light feet, despite his bulk. "This road leads to the BearHeart Logging work site, yes?"

She swallowed the dry lump in her throat. "Yes."

"Then no. I did not take a wrong turn." The cigar was returned to his mouth, the end glowed brighter before he released another cloud of smoke.

"Oh," The breathy nature of her response irritated her. She was not a simpering female, and she wasn't about to start now. Mentally, she steeled her spine. The cocky grin that irritated Rygard appeared, and she looked him up and down. "Guess you choose the wrong vehicle then, and outfit."

He growled. *Or was it a rumble?* Either way, her leopard's ears pricked up.

"It wasn't my choice of vehicle. The stupid bimbo from the temp agency filling in for my assistant placed the order with the hire car company. This..." his lip curled, he turned and stabbed the cigar at the silver Ferrari. "...Christmas bauble was waiting for me at the airport, and the F150 I wanted is not available for at least three days."

His gaze raked over her until her skin prickled with the intensity in his eyes. No amount of blue-plaid shirt was going to hide her from him, neither did the truck's window offer any refuge from his perusal.

"I'm not taking the blame for that...thing, but these roads leave much to be desired."

Stevie rolled her eyes. "It's a primary logging road. Access for loggers. Only work vehicles and haulage come up and down here. We don't need to be blacktopped." She didn't want to give him the satisfaction of agreeing with him about the road, instead she quizzed, "Why do you want BearHeart Logging?"

Cigar back in his mouth he folded his arms, the suit pulled taut across muscles that bulged with the action. "Are you Rygard Jones?"

A shake of her head would have to do. The ability to speak had left her.

"Then it's none of your business." He dismissed her, unfolded his arms, and checked his watch. "How long does it take a damn tow truck to get out here?"

Stevie shifted her weight, moving her arm from where the edge of the door was biting into her flesh. "Let's see now." She glanced skyward, determined to keep her face straight while she glibly handed the arrogant man his ass for being so rude to her. "There's only one mechanic in town with a tow truck, Pineville Nuts, Bolts, and Repairs. Assuming you rang them and spoke to Michael, you probably won't see a tow truck until tomorrow, if you are lucky."

"What?" he growled again.

Stevie clenched her thighs and silently ordered her pussy to behave. "Well, I just drove the guy who works for Michael back into town." She gave her best shit-eating grin. "Isn't it ironic that our sole mechanic comes out to site to fix a breakdown, only to have a breakdown himself before he can get back to town?"

Exasperation oozed off him as he raked one hand through his thick black hair, which caused the front of his jacket to flap, exposing a flat expanse of waist. There went the hope he was hiding a beer belly under his fancy suit. Stevie allowed herself a moment to observe his physique. He was broader than Rygard, probably taller too. A real bear of a man.

A bear of a man? That idea niggled at her mind, captured the attention of her inner cat. She opened her senses, sucking in a lungful of air and rolled his aroma around her nose and mouth. Despite the overtone of cigar smoke, he was a kick to the gut and a shot of lust straight through her core. Not to mention he was a shifter, and a formidable one at that. Notwithstanding the corporate façade, there was no mistaking the raw element of nature within him.

Her knees went weak at the idea of what he could do if he tapped into the true essence of his beast and didn't masquerade as a human.

He pinned with a baleful stare. "You'll have to take me to town. I can't stay here."

Stevie slammed back into the moment and dropped the fantasy of what he could do to her if he so chose. "Err...I don't have to do shit. I gotta get back to work, I've dawdled long enough as it is."

He pinched the bridge of his nose, brows drawn lower over his eyes than Stevie imagined possible. "Is there a cab service or ride share in town?"

She laughed. "To come out here? You gotta be kidding. I already told you, it's a primary logging road. To the landing site. No one comes out here."

"You're out here."

Stevie blinked. *Was this guy dense?* "Yeah, to get to work."

He let go of his nose and looked straight at her. "You just said this road only goes out to the logging site."

"Yeah..." Stevie let the word drop, thick with sarcasm. His expression remained blank. "You know what? Never mind.

Get in the damn truck. I'll take you with me. You wanted to see my boss anyway."

She didn't wait for him to move, just sat down, and slammed her door shut.

He moved towards the passenger side of the truck then, pulling the door open, a heavy waft of smoke floated towards her.

"Put that disgusting thing out before you get in here," she snapped. Her cat prowled around her mind, testing her control. The damn leopard was acting like she was on heat and wanted the big burly shifter to pound her into oblivion.

He complied with a glower, nipping off the burning end of the cigar before he slid into the swiftly-too-small confines of the cab. Withdrawing a gold case from his inner pocket, he clicked it open, replaced the cigar alongside the untouched ones, and shut it with a dramatic click, glaring at her askance all the while.

On the verge of retracting her offer, Stevie gritted her teeth. Everything about him overwhelmed her. He filled the truck with his body, his scent, his power. It pulsed between them, an inescapable magnetism that prickled every inch of her skin. Even her clit throbbed.

"You work for Rygard Jones?" There was suspicion in his voice.

She put the truck in gear, checked the rearview mirror then pulled out around the fancy-schmancy vehicle that had croaked. "Yeah. Have done for about three years now."

His fingers danced from the top of his thigh to his knee and back again. "You must be his secretary. No wonder my office couldn't get hold of him, if he has you shuttling mechanics around or whatever else you do to avoid answering the phone or responding to emails."

Stevie steered the passenger side of the truck closer to a pothole, jostling the arrogant prick in his seat.

His head banged the roof. "Shit."

"Sorry. Rough-ass road." She faced the other way to hide her smirk. "I'm not his secretary. Ry doesn't have one. He does his own administration. It's a little harder to keep on top of during the harvest season. There's only a small window of time to get the quota cut, hauled up to the landing, bucked, sorted, and transported. All of us have to pull our weight to get the job done, Ry too."

Now his foot bounced against the floor pan, in time with his fingers. "You know the business well?"

"I know how to do my job. I also know how hard Ry works. BearHeart Logging...it's his passion, he puts all he has into the job, into pushing the team to the limit, setting expectations, and surpassing them."

They reached the edge of the first corridor they had harvested. The light dimmed, the forest of Douglas fir soared high above them, enclosing the track almost completely.

Her passenger leaned forward, craning to see more of the trees through the windscreen. "Are these trees scheduled to be cut down?"

Stevie dragged her gaze away from the strong curve of his neck, to focus on the road. "Not for another four years. The forest is staggered in stages, these trees are allowed to grow for a minimum of sixty years before they are harvested. That section we just passed was last week's site. We're currently working another six miles along here. The next corridor isn't as wide, only half the size of the one we just passed. It's steeper though."

He looked at her, his eyes so dark they were almost black. "The forest will be replanted?"

Stevie nodded; her voice stuck in her throat at the intensity of his scrutiny. The blast of a horn startled her. The alert originated on the other side of a sharp bend in the road. She slowed the truck, pulling over to the side.

"What's wrong? What was that? Why are you stopping?"

She rolled her eyes. "Relax, pal. I'm making room for the logging truck about to come round the switch. He's bigger than me, and I don't want to screw up the turnaround time."

He snorted. "My name's Cord, not pal."

"Okay then. Good to know." Stevie rested her chin on the steering wheel, watching through the window.

Electricity zapped along her arm, arcing away from where his finger had prodded the back of her shoulder.

"It's customary to provide your own name when introductions are made, kitten."

The approaching truck was ignored, as Stevie's head whipped around, and she gave him the evil eye. "Don't call me kitten."

His lips twitched, the hint of a smile softening the harsher lines of his craggy features. "Give me your name then," he did smile then. "Kitten."

"You may call me Ms Rahal." She stuck her nose in the air, watching the tail end of the logging truck pass them bearing its load of merchantable timber.

His bark of laughter surrounded her. It annoyed her as much as it turned her on. "What? No first name for me?"

She rammed the truck into gear. "No."

He shrugged, settling in the seat until he was comfortable. "Not yet anyway."

From the corner of her eye, she caught his smirk. Her teeth clenched, but she bit back her own retort to concentrate on making sure the vehicle bumped through every blasted rut and pothole she could find. She'd shake that grin off his face before they reached the yard.

CHAPTER FIVE

CORD BUFFETT — OREGON

His day couldn't get any worse. The comedy of errors was exactly why he preferred to stay in the office and leave Benny in charge of the face-to-face work. Cord's surly nature and broody features resulted in one of two things; being hit on, or a lack of customer service.

Cooling his heels for three days so he could be his brother's best man was an added nuisance. While happy for Benny, Cord's bear had been urging him to get on with the job.

He couldn't even leave his assistant to plan his trip. The woman was called away by a family emergency. Since she was worth her weight in gold, he arranged to get her home as swiftly as possible rather than risk losing her. The temporary replacement sent by the agency had proved to be unbelievably incompetent, her ineptitude culminating in Cord's worst travel experience... ever.

His first-class seat on the aircraft was not his choice. Traffic to the airport was murder. He had arrived as the final boarding call was announced and because his nightmare assistant had checked him in online, he was unable to change his seat, meaning he had to suffer the company of several vacuous women jetting off to a fellow sorority sister's wedding. He had looked longingly through to business class as they began, clumsily, to seduce him. Travelling on daddy's money with overinflated egos, 'No' was not a word any of the gaggle had encountered.

No had been the word he hadn't wanted to accept himself when he landed and saw the ridiculous Ferrari Roma waiting for him. After a *very* heated phone call with the rep at LA Luxury Cars, he had to accept he was stuck with the obnoxious sports car for at least three days, leaving him no alternative but to suck it up and get on with the business at hand, or hole up in a hotel until the car company could deliver him a Ford F150, his preferred vehicle.

His bear wouldn't wait.

He did, however, gain a morsel of satisfaction. He had the temporary assistant fired, with a note in her file that never again was she to be employed by Buffett Property Group. His expenses were unnecessarily high, and his personal comfort forfeited because of her thoughtless decisions. Just because he was made of money, didn't mean he had to spend it.

Of course, he questioned his own decision making by not waiting for the F150, when he had set off along the gravel road leading to the BearHeart Logging work site. Unable to contact the company by phone, and given his emails had not bounced, he tracked down the office for BearHeart Logging in Pineville. Little more than a trailer on the edge of the forest, it was locked and looked as though it had been that way for some time.

"If you're looking for Rygard," a voice had called to him while he peered through grimy windows, "you'll find him out at the landing. No one from BearHeart comes into the office once they start harvesting."

Cord had swivelled to face the older shifter. "Where's that?"

The old man sniffed and spat onto the gravel. "Past the shifter boundary and into the humans' commercial forest land. Not sure why he'd want to have contracts with soulless humans but at least he's not destroying our forest in the process of playing lumberjack."

Nose turned up at the disgusting habit of the other man, Cord pressed for more information. "Could you give me the directions?"

He had pointed at Cord's hire car and laughed. "You driving that? You'll not get there in that." He shrugged. "Mind, if you're stubborn enough to try, head through town, cross the border at Muldoon's Bar, and straight on through the humans' town. The forest is signed, but the outer margins are reserved for humans who want to experience nature. Follow the signs for Pineville Falls, don't turn off there though. The logging access is the next road after that, it cuts through the reserve land into the commercial forest from there. BearHeart Logging is the only timber harvester with a contract in the area."

Cord *was* stubborn enough to follow the directions.

The Roma had bumped, scraped, and skidded its way along the access road, prompting Cord to chastise himself for not listening to the old man's caution about taking the Ferrari along a dirt track. When his front tyre blew, it took all his skill to bring the high-powered vehicle under control and over to the side of the road. His father always said his stubbornness would get him into trouble one day. Walking around the car and spotting the second flat tyre confirmed that today might just be the day he'd been warned about.

Sucking on the cigar barely took the edge off his frustrations. Waiting for the tow truck after the lackadaisical, 'he'll be there when he can,' response from the local mechanic, simply the cherry on top of his run of bad luck.

Or so he thought.

He hoped his fortunes might be changing for the better when the young woman turned up. She confused him, hiding behind the open door of the truck, a baseball cap covering most of her hair, her shape concealed beneath a baggy blue-plaid shirt buttoned to her collar bone. From what he spied of her graceful neck, she looked to be blessed with flawless, olive toned skin.

Upon learning the tow truck wouldn't pick him up before tomorrow, he had demanded she give him a lift, guessing — by the way he was being thrown around in his seat — she was offended by his attitude.

She had intrigued him with her evasive answers about her role at BearHeart Logging. Her atrocious driving, snaking back and forth along the road, clipping every divot in the road, did little to endear her to him.

Cord bit down on his bear's headspace. She didn't need to endear herself to him. He wasn't interested in her, ignoring the fact her natural perfume enticed him and stirred his lust.

She wasn't his type. He couldn't visualise her wearing a Roberto Cavalli skin-tight dress and Louboutin pumps. Yet he couldn't stop his gaze veering in her direction. Noting how her slender fingers grasped the steering wheel or cradled the knob of the gear stick. He shifted in his seat, his pants becoming rather too snug for comfort.

His teeth rattled in his head as, travelling a little too fast, the car jostled over a series of corrugations on the road. His lust subsided. "How much further?"

Toot-toot

She jerked her chin forwards, eyes fixed straight ahead. "Hear that? That's the whistler. Not far now, or you wouldn't hear it."

Listening, he picked up on the various machines working ahead, they melded together in such a cacophony, he wasn't surprised by the bustling scene which met his eyes when they rounded the corner.

Ms Rahal pointed the truck between two parked vehicles. Cord jolted forward when she hit the brakes and killed the engine.

"Come on, time's money," she chirped, leaning between the seats to grab a hard hat, the yellow paint scratched to reveal the silver surface below.

Cord realised how small she was when she alighted, slammed the door, and marched off. He hastened after her.

Despite the uneven ground and Ms Rahal's heavy work boots, she moved with grace. Her shirttail was tucked into the back of her jeans giving him a clear view of her perfect ass. He shook his head and hurried to catch up with her. His Italian loafers might look sharp in the boardroom, but they were totally unsuitable for the deep wheel ruts in the dried mud he had to negotiate. Jaw taut, he ignored the unease sliding along the back of his neck, and the damage he imagined was being inflicted on the soft leather of his shoes.

"Stevie. Baby." A deep voice hailed her from across the work site.

A tall, lanky man jumped down from the cab of one of the big machines, his long strides eating up the distance between him and the woman in front of Cord. He wrapped his brawny hands around her rib cage, pulling the shirt she wore tight enough to reveal a slim figure. He lowered his head but, the kiss Cord was sure the guy hoped to steal was forestalled by her hand.

"Not at work, Ry. We talked about this," she hissed.

A hint of colour crept across the other man's face, and he released her. "Yeah, sorry."

Cord bit back a snigger. Witnessing the other man's submission to the tiny woman extinguished his inexplicable spike of jealously.

The other man's head snapped up, dark eyes meeting Cord's. "Who's the stiff you brought out, ba...Stevie?"

Stevie. Cord's lips twitched. The name suited her, from the yellow hard hat on her head to the scuffed safety boots on her feet. He wanted to know what her name sounded like rolling off his tongue.

Arms crossed, hip cocked out to one side, she tipped her head in his direction. "I rescued his sorry ass from the side of the road."

He scowled, all desire to sample her name on his tongue quashed by her impudence. "My former assistant screwed up the hire car." He glared at Stevie, noting her brown eyes dancing with a mischievous light.

Stevie looked at the other man. "He wants to see you, Ry. Has a bone to pick with your secretary, or rather lack thereof because he can't speak to you without venturing into the wilds of the forest."

"Rygard Jones?" queried Cord. His curiosity piqued when the other man, almost as tall as he, just not as wide in his frame nodded. So, this was his blood father's other son. He extended his hand. "Cord Buffett, CEO of Buffett Property Group."

Rygard placed his hand in Cord's. His grip was firm but lacked any underlying challenge.

Deliberately, Cord squeezed the younger man's hand. His bear surged forward within his mind, and it was all Cord could do to rein him back in.

The younger man broke eye contact first, submitting almost instantly to the unintentional leak of alpha power. "Yeah? What can I do for you?"

"I wanted to talk busine—"

Metal screeched.

"Look out," the yell could hardly be heard over the din.

Stevie shot off across the ground to bounce up onto one log, then another, darting over the shifting stack of timber. She launched into the air, catapulting herself against another body, both disappearing into the stack of wood spilling over the crest of the hill.

The boom arm of a machine swung out and down, anchoring the wood before it could slide any further.

All work ground to a halt, and the noise of the machinery faded into absolute silence.

"Stevie! Jas!"

Rygard bolted towards the pile of timber.

"We're here," A voice hailed them from within the pile. "I'm okay, but Jason's hat got knocked off and he was hit on the head, he's out for the count."

Cord followed, unsure what to do, but his bear roared within his mind. He needed to help Stevie.

"Get that big stick loader over here," ordered Rygard. "We gotta get this off them now. Where are you, Stevie?" He ran along the top edge of the timber, searching for her.

Something yellow moved in a gap in the wood. "I see her," shouted Cord, racing towards the siding. He reached his hand into the giant game of Sticks, gratified to feel small fingers clutch his larger ones. Sparks coursed through him at her touch. "She's here."

A hand landed on Cord's shoulder, hauling him away from the pile, and ripping his hand from Stevie's. He wanted to growl in protest, but the other men had the tools necessary to secure the wood and pull the logs up.

He was pushed out the way by the experienced lumberjacks. They were a well-oiled machine, working together to extract Stevie and a dazed looking young male.

Rygard hoisted Stevie out of the wood pile and into his arms, knocking off her hard hat in the process. "You okay, baby?"

"Yeah. I'm fine, Ry, but you gotta help Jas out. He probably needs a healer." Stevie tried to wriggle free.

"I'm fine, Stevie," Jas assured her, currently being helped from the pile. "You saved me from getting crushed by forcing us into that gap. Thanks, mate."

He swayed on his feet as the other men assisted him onto solid ground. An older version of Jason placed on hand on his shoulder, and the other round his jaw, compelling Jas to look at him. "You got a nasty gash on your head, son. Eyes look a little glazed too."

"Fuck." Rygard scratched at the back of his neck, finally allowing Stevie to put space between them. "Timmo, you take Jas back to town, get him checked out. Don't let him come back until the healer clears him for work. Everyone else, let's get this pile re-stacked then we'll call it for the day."

Stevie scrambled off the wood, moving more slowly now than she had when she sprinted towards the slide.

Cord reached for her as she passed him, letting his hand drop when she avoided him. He wasn't sure why he had tried to touch her. His bear careened around in his head, making it ache.

Rygard approached. "Give me an hour to oversee this stack, and I'll get you back to town where we can talk."

Cord nodded; his eyes fixed on Stevie who was checking the injured man being settled into the passenger seat of another truck.

When she stepped back, Rygard's hand came to rest on her nape. He was laying claim to her. Making it clear to everyone, especially Cord, that Stevie was his woman.

The bear roared within Cord, thumping against the mental walls holding him in place. Stevie would be his. Just as Rygard's mother had stolen their father from Cord's mother, Cord would steal Stevie from Rygard.

Sins of the mother, paid for by the son. There was a poetic justice to it, Cord was certain.

CHAPTER SIX

STEVIE RAHAL — OREGON

Her skin crawled. Stevie rubbed at her neck, expecting to find a colony of little black ants marching across her shoulders. Sweat pooled under her short nails with each scratch. No ants.

Rygard had her trapped against the high table where she sat in Muldoon's bar with the rest of the BearHeart crew. He dipped his head, running his nose along the skin behind her ear.

Stevie pushed his head back. "Eww, I'm filthy from work, get away."

"You smell good to me, babe. Like sweat and sawdust all rolled into one." He moved in again.

"No, I need a shower before you get all up in my personal space." She shoved his head harder, digging the heel of her hand into his nose. "What's with the sudden displays of public affection, anyway?"

He glanced around the table, scanning every bear shifter who worked for him. Only Timmo and Jas were absent. Shrugging, he sat in the empty seat next to Stevie. "Can't a guy show his woman what she means to him, especially when she was nearly crushed?"

She almost choked on her mouthful of beer. "Excuse me?" Incredulous, Stevie leaned back. "I'm not your woman, Ry."

Sniggers ghosted around the table, quelled only by the sharp glare Rygard slashed across the men.

Stevie sucked in a deep breath before she stood, her heels hooked over the footrest of the bar stool, adding inches to her height. She whispered in Rygard's ear. "We agreed, Ry. Just jokes. Fun and games, that's all. We're not mates, remember."

His hand sought under her shirt; his thumb skimmed over the bare skin above the waistband of her work jeans. "Are you so sure?"

She rocked back, thighs hitting the smooth seat of the bar stool. Stevie blinked. "What?" She shook her head. "I'm going to the throne room."

Bobo laughed. "You mean the little sows' room, Stevie?"

Stevie flipped him the bird and got off her stool. "No, Bobo. The throne room, I'm a queen after all, remember."

Laughter followed her across the room, the tension from the awkward encounter between Rygard and Stevie broken by the banter. She wove her way through the empty tables towards the rear hallway. It was too early for the bar to be full, but there was still a smattering of bear shifters huddled together, even a human or two.

Her mind whirled faster than her Husky's chain. For months she had been enjoying sexual benefits with Rygard, scratching an itch, getting laid without the hassles men brought with their strings attached. She'd been clear from the start. She wasn't in it for the long haul, she only wanted a good time, and until today, she was certain he had accepted that. His unexpected about face, paired with his public displays of possessiveness, irked her. Stevie sighed as mentally she made a note to stock up on batteries. If Rygard didn't fall back into line, she'd be sating her cat's libido with battery power once more.

The door at the end of the narrow corridor opened. A gust of wind whipped through like a tunnel, chilling her skin and mussing her hair. Surprised to realise she was at the other side of the bar already; Stevie brushed the stray strands of hair out of her eyes and came face to face with Cord.

He snapped his gold cigar case shut at the same time the door banged closed behind him. His eyes gleamed under the artificial glow of the ceiling light. The fluorescent strip flicked a moment before it dimmed, enclosing the pair in a gloomy space.

Her heart beat a rapid tattoo, blood thundered in her ears, and her breathing hitched. Stevie's cat purred, supplying plenty of sordid imagery of her curved around the strapping man.

Cord stared down at her, his bulk almost filling the hallway, as he surveyed her body lazily.

Stevie shivered. He was stripping her layers away one by one, laying her bare for his leisurely perusal. Her stomach tightened, heat coiling under his predatory gleam. Her lips parted; a shallow breath slipped past dry lips. "I—" her voice caught in her throat.

She pointed to the door behind him on the right. With a cough she cleared her throat enough to croak, "Restroom."

The corner of his mouth quirked. The inner light of his animal danced in his eyes as he stood aside, giving her scarcely enough room to pass.

Eyes fixed on the imposing man; Stevie had a choice. *Did she squeeze past facing him, or with her back to him?* Wracked with indecision she opted to face the wall, closing her eyes when she shuffled by. Heat engulfed her, crashing over her back and battering her senses. He never moved, didn't even attempt to grab her ass. She had no alternative but to brush against him, her butt grazing his solid thighs. She might as well be naked for the level of sensation searing her skin from even so slight a contact.

Stevie's cat bombarded her with myriad images. Large hands dwarfing her hips as he moulded her flush to him. Her pliant body filled with his heat, his essence, his seed. Succumbing to his domination — something no man had ever achieved before.

Her lip caught between her teeth, Stevie bit back a moan and rushed for the door to the restroom. It swung open under her hand, and she burst into the brightly lit space. The pungent scent of bleach and artificial lavender smacked her in the nose and cleansed the cigar and sandalwood from her senses. The door shut, and Stevie's head thudded against the polished surface, as she attempted to knock the lust-ridden imagery from her mind adding a couple of extra thuds for good measure.

She released a shaky breath she didn't know she'd been holding, flexed her arms, cracked her neck, and entered the nearest stall.

"Get it together, girl," she murmured as she went about her business. "He's just a guy. Just a... tall... solid... good looking... guy." She shook her head as she stood then flushed. She needed Rygard to take her home and scratch her itch.

Stevie groaned as she fastened her belt. *Was Rygard going to get clingy if she took him home now?* She washed her hands, watching the suds swirl around the basin and down the plug hole. Turning off the tap, she met her reflection in the mirror.

Her dark brown eyes didn't look any different, they were still framed by the same thick lashes. Her cat couldn't be seen in her eyes, despite her feisty presence in Stevie's mind. She scoffed at herself. "So stupid." *What did she expect? To see the tawny creature stalking back and forth in her pupils?*

The door swung open. Stevie spun to face the door.

"Are you okay, Stephanie?" Rygard's mother, Magda walked in.

"Stevie," she corrected softly. "I'm fine, Madga. You caught me by surprise, is all. It's so quiet in the bar, I never expected anyone else to come in."

The older woman pinned Stevie with an assessing gaze, then her ageless face cleared of all expression, and she canted her head. "Ummm. I didn't expect to find Rygard's crew here at this time of day, if I am honest."

Stevie shrugged. "There was an incident at the landing. Jas was hurt. Ry gave us the afternoon off rather than put the team at more risk working with two men down."

Magda sniffed. "Sensible, I suppose."

The two women side-stepped each other to avoid contact as they swapped places. Despite the unease Stevie experienced around the Torben alpha's mate, she couldn't keep her mouth shut.

"Isn't it a little early for you to be here, Magda?" Stevie paused, fingers on the door handle, the door ajar.

Magda looked over her shoulder, her thick red hair, streaked with white, cascaded down her back as she retorted, "I have a business meeting. Not that you needed to know that."

Stevie dipped her head in attempt to placate the temperamental she-bear. "You're right. Sorry." She wrenched the door open and scampered out as quickly as possible.

In the hallway, she lifted her head, eyes burning as she stared into the fluorescent light, which had brightened again.

Home.

Between the emotionally unstable she-bear and the intensely broody male who revved up her libido, Stevie knew she would be safer at home.

Steadying herself, she headed back to the main section of the bar. A few more shifters had trickled in, the hum of conversation buzzed a little louder than it had earlier.

Laughter erupted from the BearHeart Logging crew, drinks flowing freely as they enjoyed a rare afternoon off during the height of harvest season.

Without consciously searching for him, Stevie's attention was drawn to the small table in a shadowy corner of the bar. Cord dominated the space, his very presence rippled with an unspoken superiority, which created a natural barrier between him and the other occupants of Muldoon's bar.

His head lifted, dark eyes fathomless, even from across the room, as he met her gaze. He said nothing, yet the way he raised his whiskey glass in her direction, spoke volumes. The deep amber liquid sloshed with the gesture, splashing over the rim onto his fingers.

Stevie licked her lips. Her cat whispered something about lapping the liquor from his skin.

As though reading her mind, his mouth twisted into a half smirk. He lifted his hand, bowed his head and, locking his gaze on her, sucked his hand.

Heat unfurled in her belly, her clit tingled, and desire speared through her body. He might as well have just fastened his mouth over her pussy rather than his hand for the way she reacted. Her mouth dropped open and she panted.

"For heaven's sake, Stephanie. Stop loitering."

Magda's sharp voice in her ear ruined the moment. Cord lowered his hand, his expression soured, and Stevie whirled around to face the older woman.

"What?" she husked, blinking at the woman's churlish expression.

Red painted lips thinned, revealing the lines of age around her mouth, her forehead furrowed, until, on a huff, her face smoothed out. "You're blocking the way, Stephanie. Could you please move aside?"

Stevie stepped back, her butt bumping the edge of a nearby table. "What? Oh. Yes. Sorry, Magda."

Narrowed green eyes flashed, as Magda flipped her hair over her shoulder, straightened her white silk blouse scattered with red roses, and strutted across the room like she owned the place.

Stevie watched her go; her stare fixed on the emphasised sway of ample hips. She had never understood why Magda rubbed her cat up the wrong way. She presented as a human, the scent of bear more of a familial connection around her. Stevie had not witnessed the woman shift. Rygard's father, on the other hand, as far as she knew, spent all his days as a bear.

Her cat snarled within her, watching as the red head slid into the seat beside Cord, her hand touching his as she spoke to him. Stevie dug her nails into her palms. Dismissing a proprietorial pang, she dodged around the tables until she reached her crew's table.

"What'd I miss?"

Rygard shifted in his seat, snaked one arm around her and pulled her into his side. "Timmo just called. Jas will be fine. The healer said he has a hard head with no serious damage. Bed rest for a day while he recovers from the concussion, but he'll be good as new after that."

Stevie's skin itched at Rygard's possessive gesture. With a nonchalant roll of her shoulders, his arm slipped off. "That's good news. I guess, since we'll be working a man short tomorrow, I'll have an early night. I wanna sharpen my Husky and get everything ready for the morning. Night guys."

Downing his drink, Rygard stood. "I'll drive you home."

Stevie shook her head. The idea of spending the night with Rygard no longer appealed. "No need, Ry. I'll walk. Stretch out the kinks after that mad tumble through the stack."

He frowned. "Babe—"

She grinned. "It's all good, Paddington—"

"Don't call me that," he groused, plonking back onto his seat.

Stevie winked and continued to speak over the surly bear-shifter. "—Bear. The walk will do me good." She nodded at her smirking work mates, set her sights firmly on the entrance, and stiffened her neck. She would not look, refused to look.

Shit... she looked.

Cord met her gaze. His dark eyes followed her every move until she slipped out into the cooler air.

Stevie pressed trembling fingertips to her burning cheeks. No male had ever captured her attention so thoroughly that even her leopard rubbed up against her mental walls determined to break free and wind herself around the man in question. With a light smack to her forehead, she shook off the urge to walk back into Muldoon's, climb into Cord's lap and take him where he sat, patrons of the bar be damned.

Stevie stomped to the work vehicle. Standing on tiptoes on the top of the rear tyre, her stomach digging into the side of the tray, she stretched over to grab her chainsaw. With a grunt she hoisted it over her shoulder and, carefully, climbed down to the asphalt of the lot. Adjusting the balance of the heavy machine, she set off through the slowly filling parking lot towards the road out of town.

She gave her cat a stern talking to about getting all worked up over a stranger — a broody, yuppie of a man at that — as she walked home, ascribing the prickling of her nape to the residual effects of her cat's lust for Cord.

She ignored the echo of a heavier step following her as she moved away from the safety of town.

CHAPTER SEVEN

CORD BUFFETT — OREGON

S tevie beguiled him. She was the opposite of anything he looked for in a woman. She barely reached the middle of his chest; the shapeless clothes did little to show off her figure — if she even had one — but her olive skin and dark hair enchanted him. He wanted to peel away the flannel shirt and divest her of the heavy denim. He wanted to see whether she was curvy, toned or stick thin. His bear battered against his self-control. He wanted the woman, roared to take her, in fact.

Both Cord and his bear agreed that Rygard didn't deserve to touch her. He wasn't man enough, not bear enough, not alpha enough to tame the mile-wide wild streak that was Stevie. She was all sass and mouth. Cord cleared his throat, smothering a smile at how he could put that mouth to better use.

When he encountered her in the corridor at the back of the bar, it took every ounce of self-discipline to keep his hands to himself. He wanted to haul her up, slam her against the wall and fill her repeatedly until she screamed his name.

He'd been rock hard when she edged past him, her tight ass brushing his thighs, teasing the tip of his cock barely restrained in his pants.

She had shot into the restroom like a scalded cat. The deafening bang of the door had broken the spell ensnaring him. Needing a moment, he straightened his tie and adjusted the cuffs of his jacket, then entered the bar.

Muldoon jerked his head, gaining Cord's attention.

"Alp..." Muldoon choked on his words, cleared his throat and started again. "Cord. Did you settle in okay?"

Cord's brows knitted, and he shook his head. "Got the damn hire car stuck on the access road to BearHeart Logging's work site."

Muldoon's gawked. "Say what now? Why did you go out there? I thought you were just going to be dealing with," his face pinched, "Magda."

The seams of Cord's jacket strained as he crossed his arms. "My business is none of yours, old man."

The light of his inner bear brightened behind Muldoon's eyes, cutting through the mist of age. "As an elder, if your actions are going to effect the Tribe, it *is* my business, young man."

The two men stared each other down. Being around other shifters was a new experience for Cord. He wasn't used to the heightened senses of his bear detecting the subtle nuances in expression, scent, and body language. Cord was the businessman. Shrewd, some in the industry even called him a shark for the predatory practises he employed when it came to expanding the Buffett Property Group, especially when that expansion absorbed smaller, weaker businesses.

Muldoon conceded first. His eyes widened briefly before flickering behind Cord. He cleared his throat. "Magda."

"Muldoon."

Cord recognised the contrived cordiality in the greeting. He'd been around enough people in his line of work to know when an individual presented one façade, while hiding another. It made him good at his job. His ground his molars then steeled himself to face the woman for the first time.

Her bright green eyes were framed with heavily mascaraed lashes, her pouting lips stained red by a thick matte lipstick. She was everything he hated in a woman; her features disguised behind the artifice of make-up. Her bright white, straight teeth gleamed as she feigned a welcoming smile. "You must be Cord Buffett."

He inclined his head, "Yes, ma'am."

A flash of irritation chased across her face before she reacted. "Magda, please. Ma'am makes me sound old enough to be your mother!"

Cord lifted a brow. *Was the woman delusional?* "You actually are," he muttered, *sotto voce*, before clearing his throat. "Magda it is." His throat tightened around the name, but he hadn't made it to where he was in life without playing nice with people far nastier than the wannabe cougar in front of him.

Her lips pursed, and her overly friendly smile dulled. "Would you excuse me a moment? It seems I need to freshen up."

Cord gave a curt nod and looked at Muldoon. "Scotch, neat."

With a dip of his head, Muldoon, shuffled to a cupboard, half hidden behind the row of fridges. He bent down to swing it open and retrieved a bottle of Macallan. "I keep the good stuff out of the way. Not many folks in these parts have a palate cultured enough to appreciate the refined flavours of a good whiskey."

Cord cleared his throat. "That was ma's favourite. We always drink it in her memory."

"Well let's have one together for Lizzie." Muldoon's voice was husky as he put the bottle on the bar mat.

"Sure. Then just give me Walker Blue for the rest of the night."

The generous measures of Scotch were poured into squat, crystal-cut tumblers. Muldoon recapped and replaced the bottle, then lifted one glass, his gaze on Cord.

Cord didn't take the second glass. Images of his mother reared up in his mind. Those lighter moments, her face bright with laughter, love radiating from her as she cradled Benny in her arms while Abe held her. Darker memories smashed through the happier ones. Lizzie's fear and sadness. Her face closed; arms hugging her body. The vision seen through his bear's eyes after his first shift.

She had never looked at him in the same way again. Lizzie Buffett had loved him, demonstrated in her smile and the special ruffle of his hair, but Cord knew, the older he got, the bigger he grew, the more his bear influenced his pubescent temperament, the greater the distance between his mother and him. The more she recalled haunting moments from her youth, the more she feared him, and it broke his heart.

Muldoon nudged the glass of Macallan towards Cord.

Anger fuelled Cord. He took the Scotch from the old bear-shifter.

"To Lizzie."

"Mother." Cord stared into the ruby-hued liquid as he made his mental vow. *I will kill the bear and the bitch who hurt you, I promise.*

The glasses chinked together and both men downed the contents. The silky-smooth glide of the Scotch fired up Cord. The flavour dancing on his tongue teased him with the plans of revenge. He would destroy the Jones family. He would topple the Torben tribe. Everyone would pay for the dread in his mother's eyes every time she saw his bear.

Muldoon cleared his throat. "Right. Johnnie Walker Blue coming up."

Cord lifted his gaze from the empty glass. He needed to drown out his inner bear. Assuage the beast long enough to initiate the moves he had plotted out for the long game. "Keep them coming while I am here, old man."

Muldoon nodded, refilling Cord's glass from the square-edged bottle of Johnnie Walker.

Full glass in hand, Cord strode back to the small table in the shadowy corner of the bar. It offered a sense of privacy, a modicum of control. Cord might not be in the familiar setting of a boardroom, but he was the one holding the winning hand. He was certain. Magda Jones had no idea she was about to be played.

He had barely settled into his seat when his chest pinched. He glanced up, to see Stevie. She held his stare with her wide brown eyes. Colour crept across her tanned skin, highlighting her delicate cheekbones. Her chest rose and fell with her sharp breaths. She wasn't immune to him, he was sure.

Cord saluted the feisty little shifter with his glass. He wasn't sure of her inner creature, but she was too small to be a bear. Every female shifter he had so far encountered, and he hadn't been in town long, from the Torben tribe were almost as tall as their male counterparts, with curvier hips.

Scotch splashed against his hand, the liquid cool against the heat of his skin.

He noticed Stevie's mouth fall open and watched her tongue sweep across her lower lip.

He couldn't prevent the smirk, even had he wanted to. With cocky deliberation, he swirled his tongue over the Scotch. A tacit declaration of his intent the moment he got her into his bed. And he *would* have her in his bed, for once, he and his bear agreed on that score; Stevie captivated and intrigued both man and beast.

That she was Rygard's woman, merely a bonus. He would take her from him. Hurt him, the way Rygard's mother had hurt Cord's mother. Regardless that Rygard was younger and an innocent pawn, the scrawny, pathetic excuse for an alpha male was guilty by association.

Magda appeared behind Stevie, breaking the spell. Stevie moved aside, allowing room for the older woman to strut across the bar. Cord threw back his head, swallowing down the Scotch in his glass rather than watch the sway of Magda's hips, disgusted by the way she tried to seduce him. She was a mated woman.

A cloud of flowery perfume assailed him. *Was Magda wearing that when she first approached him, or had she applied the cloying stuff in the restroom?* He lowered his head, and the glass clunked onto the table.

Magda flipped her hair over her shoulder and sat next to him. "So, Cord, tell me about yourself." Long, red-painted nails traced the top of his hand still gripping the glass.

It took all his self-control not to shift and batter the woman who dared touch him to a pulp. The woman who had traumatised his mother, so badly, she was scarred for life, despite being loved and cherished by Abe Buffett.

"I'm the CEO of Buffett Property Group. I took over from my father six years ago, when he chose to retire." Cord grunted a half laugh, "at least that's what he tells everyone.

He maintains a close eye on the family business, working more hours in a week than any retiree should."

Magda rolled her eyes. "I don't want your corporate bio, Cord. I want to hear more about you."

Cord removed his hand from under Magda's talons, using the gesture to check the time, only to have his attention caught by Stevie crossing the bar.

As though sensing his scrutiny, Stevie looked at him, holding his eyes until she disappeared out of Muldoon's.

Clearing his throat, Cord swung his gaze back to Magda. "We really ought to get down to business. I have another meeting in an hour."

She stiffened, her breasts pushing forward. "With who? I run this town."

"Oh? According to the Better Business Bureau you don't own every business in Pineville."

Magda deflated, then straightened, tapping a manicured nail on the tabletop. "True, but the Torben tribe owns the title to over ninety percent of the businesses in Pineville."

Cord flashed his teeth with a smile that never reached his eyes. "And I have a contract for the sale of those businesses ready for you to sign."

Magda lifted a hand to toy with the tiger's eye pendant resting at the swell of her breasts. "Remind me, why we should sell our businesses to you? We never put them on the market. Out of the blue, someone from your office approached me, offering to buy us out. I researched

Buffet Property Group. All your previous business has been conducted in California. You have a reputation as well, you know."

Cord studied the woman through hooded eyes. "I agree, BPG does have a reputation, but we are not as ruthless as some disgruntled people would have others believe. BPG started as a modest real estate business. Homes and business spaces for rent, eventually branching out to building and selling homes. Since I took over from my father, we have started acquiring property or businesses which are failing. After a thorough audit of the prospective business's current practices, we replace either some or all the board members before injecting the companies with a renewed cash flow, training the existing staff with better skills until they become profitable commodities once more. Some boards make the choice to remain under the BPG umbrella, others, once back on their feet, redeem their titles from us."

A foot rubbed against Cord's ankle, snagging on the material of his pants before sliding higher up his leg. "And how does that little history lesson in your savvy business practices relate to this backwards little shifter town of Pineville, Oregon?"

Cord moved his leg away from the unwanted intrusion on his personal space. With a shrug, he rattled off the story he had crafted for such a question. "It was time to branch out, I don't want the company to be restricted to California. I tasked my team with finding businesses and properties which met certain criteria. Pineville checked most if not all the boxes." Cord leaned forward on to his elbows, his fingers crossed just under his nose. "Let's be honest, Magda. Your town — your tribe, they are haemorrhaging money. If you continue at the rate you are, the Torben tribe will be bankrupt before the end of next year. Your alpha is failing the tribe, tromping about through the woods as a bear twenty-four hours a day, seven days a week. How does a mindless beast lead his people?"

Magda narrowed her eyes, and Cord saw her fingers whiten around the stone at her neck. "I govern the tribe in his place."

He sat back and fastened his hands behind his head, his shirt stretching taut across his chest. "Which is why I am speaking with you now. I think you'll find the remuneration package I am offering to the tribe very lucrative."

Arching a brow, Magda stroked a nail under the rim of her lower lip. "Just how much are we talking about?"

Cord pulled a gold pen from inside his jacket. Flipping over the beer mat in front of him, he scrawled a figure. Capping his pen, he returned it to his pocket and pushed the mat towards Magda with his index finger.

She gaped, saucer-eyed at the number of zeros.

CHAPTER EIGHT

STEVIE RAHAL — OREGON

S tevie was so close. Teetering on the brink. A little nudge and she could soar, an orgasm crashing through her. Every time she was close to coming, keening with the build-up, *his* face, his brooding gaze boring into her, floated behind her closed eyes, and the zing of her peak fizzled away, dissipating without so much as a pop. Her head fell back against the bed, her cat rumbling at the lack of gratification.

Stevie had been chasing an orgasm for at least half an hour. Her arm was numb, and her elbow, painfully stiff from angling the vibrator just so. Stabbing the button with her thumb, she switched off the dying toy. If it couldn't get her over the edge with full power, nearly-dead batteries wouldn't give her what she needed.

She was wet. Oh, so wet.... and empty. With only a clitoral stimulation toy on hand, she would stay empty. Usually, it was enough for her to get off, to sate her leopard.

Tonight, she couldn't get anywhere, leaving her more frustrated than before she had given up on trying to sleep. She needed more, needed to be filled. The vibrating dildo she brought with her to Pineville was a dud, dying the week she bought it. She hadn't had a chance to return to Salem to replace it. There was no way she would even attempt an online delivery, let alone buy a sex toy in a small town like Pineville, where everyone knew everyone's business — regardless of which side of town.

When she first arrived in Pineville, Stevie was surprised to find how slight the divide was between the two species. Timmo had discussed it at length with her, one night when he taught her how to maintain her chainsaw. The segregation between shifter and human had started to blur after Magda, born human, had mated with the tribe's alpha, Ryan Jones. The older generations of the town maintained the distinction, but Stevie's contemporaries were comfortable interacting with those on the human side of the town.

A lot of families had left the Torben tribe, selling their homes and businesses to the alpha and the council of elders. The tribe was weakening. The invisible and once inviolable barrier between shifter and human was crumbling, causing a frisson of unease among Timmo's peers, who had tried to bridge the gap between the elders and the younger members.

The humans, of course, while content to acknowledge the existence of shifters, stayed on their side of town. Ninety percent of the town's businesses and properties were owned by humans who conveniently forgot there was a little more to Pineville once you passed Muldoon's bar.

Stevie reached for her phone. No new messages. Rygard hadn't replied to her booty call, and it wasn't like him to ignore her when she invited him over to play. She exhaled a long, slow breath and hit the button to call the playful bear. Although he had made her uncomfortable on site, and again at Muldoon's, but he was a red-blooded male who came with what she desperately needed. A hard cock.

The call rang out. The robotic voice of the standard answer service echoed through her phone. Well, dammit all, if he wouldn't come to her, she would go to him. She tossed her phone in disgust, and it skidded across the mattress as she jumped out of bed. She pulled on yoga pants without panties, slipped her favourite kaftan over her head, and fastened her sandals.

"Shit." Stevie was halfway down the stairs when she remembered her cell. Retracing her steps, she picked up the phone — she would forget her head if it wasn't screwed on — grinning as she descended the stairs. "I seriously need to get off. Especially if I can't even remember how to cum, or even take my phone with me."

She *did* remember to take a breath as the door closed behind her. The honey-almond-vanilla fragrance of the night phlox lured her, tempting her to stay awhile and admire the white and purple flowers blooming under the moon. She trailed her fingers over the velvet soft petals as she passed, releasing more of the sweet aroma into the air.

Exiting her rambling little garden, Stevie marched with intent to Rygard's place. He had better be home because, if she had to return home without him answering her booty call, he would suffer more than a cold shoulder.

The five-mile walk did little to settle her nerves. In fact, by the time she turned into the cul-de-sac where Rygard lived, she was more on edge than before she left home. Her cat prowled in her mind, agitated by every noise that reached Stevie's ears.

Her father would have said evil lurked nearby. Nothing good ever came from the bad intentions of others, especially if they happened to be potent enough to influence the intrinsic elements of the night, causing the fur of their leopards to bristle and their minds to hiss.

"You're being unreasonable."

The voice drifting on the breeze, prickled with familiarity. Cigar smoke wafted towards her, overpowering the residual scent of night phlox lingering on her fingers.

Her clit pulsed. Unbidden, a vision of Cord, his dark head between her legs rose in her mind. The stubble of his jaw scratching at the soft skin between her thighs as his tongue delved into her pussy.

"BearHeart Logging is mine. Why would you want to take that from me?" Rygard's petulant tone, smashed through the steamy scene taunting Stevie.

Stevie slowed her pace, creeping up behind the hedge that marked the boundary of Rygard's property from the public footpath.

Cord's laugh held no mirth. "You might know what you are doing when it comes to felling, stacking, and selling timber, but your business operation is a shambles. Have you any idea how many times I called and emailed trying to contact you? Not counting those made by my office. Your publicly declared financials have you barely breaking even on costs. The only sensible option is for you to sell to Buffett Property Group."

Stevie slapped a hand across her mouth to silence her noise of protest unaware neither of the two men would have heard her over Rygard's curse.

"What do *you* want with a logging company, Cali boy?"

Cord's growl resonated deep in Stevie's core. Lord, if he did that right on her clit she'd fall apart at the seams, let alone fall off the peak she'd been chasing all night!

"The price of lumber is skyrocketing; it makes sense for my company to invest in timber companies. We build houses, you harvest a valuable material used in that process."

Rygard snorted. "So, you reduce costs by cutting out the middleman. What do I get out of the deal?"

"You wouldn't have to worry about the administration of the business. I would have a team sent here to manage that side of the operation. You get an influx of cash, and a guaranteed price for your harvest, at a higher rate than you currently receive. Honestly, with cutting out the various middlemen, my costs would still be cheaper buying direct from BearHeart Logging."

"Why not just negotiate a contract to buy all my lumber? Why do I have to sell the business to you?"

"Because if you continue the way you are, currently, BearHeart Logging will be bankrupt in less than two years. I'll be back to square one, and you will have lost your passion. What will you do then? Step up and be alpha?"

"My father—"

"Is a mindless bear. He lost his humanity years ago. What do you think he will do for your tribe?"

"My mother—"

"That whore has run the tribe almost into the ground."

There was a loud clatter, Stevie peeked around the corner of the hedge.

Rygard's chair had toppled backwards, and he stood over Cord. "What did you call my mother?"

Cord removed the cigar from his mouth and exhaled a thick cloud of smoke into Rygard's face. "You heard me, pup."

Something cracked behind Stevie.

Rygard snarled, "Bastard."

At the same time, a large hand clamped around the top of her arm, swinging her up and away from the hedge.

She screamed.

She was hanging just above the ground. Her shoulder was numb, fingers digging in on either side of the ball joint.

She writhed, trying to kick the hulk as he marched through Rygard's front gate.

"Stevie?" Releasing Cord's shirt, Rygard moved towards the edge of the deck. "Who the hell are you? What are you doing with my girl?"

"*Your* girl?" The guy holding her let out a sardonic laugh. "I'd keep a better eye on *my* mate. No way I'd let her walk home from a bar alone. I certainly wouldn't leave her so needy that even her toys can't get her off."

Stevie stopped struggling and went limp.

Her cat snarled within her, pushing forward to regain some semblance of control. "You, filthy pervert," she hissed, swivelling in his clutches, her feet striking his ribs.

He lost his grip, and Stevie slithered to the ground, landing on her hands and knees.

A large foot pressed her down, grinding her hips into the gravel of Rygard's footpath. Spittle sprayed her nape when he crowed, "Feisty little wild cat, aren't you? Now stay still while I stake my claim."

"What do you want?"

Stevie arched her neck, looking up to see Rygard stomp down the deck steps. Cord was still in his seat, cigar between his lips. Guardedly, he folded back the sleeves of his shirt, exposing rugged forearms, dusted with dark hair.

"What are you going to do, little alpha?" sneered the man above Stevie. "Run home to mommy and ask the witch to cast a spell on me? Better yet, you want to call big daddy in from the woods to fight your battles for you?"

"I don't need anyone to fight my battles." Rygard reached for the axe lodged in a block of wood. With a practised twist, he slid the blade free.

Several pairs of large, bare feet filed past Stevie to stand in a loose semi-circle in front of Rygard's home. She couldn't see much from her prone position, but from the size of their calf muscles, running up to sinewy thighs which disappeared under baggy shorts, all appeared to be strapping males.

Rygard swung the axe onto his shoulder. "Seems you can't fight your own battles though; you need your thugs." He frowned and pointed the axe at a male to his right. "I know you. Your younger brother was in my class at school. You're a Torben bear."

The heel on Stevie's back, pushed her deeper into the gravel, as the man above her adjusted his weight. "We all were, until your bitch of a mother sank her witchy claws into the alpha and turned him into her own personal sex-slave. Shifters were never meant to be so cosy with humans, and he should never have given that woman the time of day, let alone kept fucking her until she had him wrapped around her little finger!"

Another glob of spittle landed near Stevie's head.

"We all watched as she drugged him, adding more and more of her herbs and seeds and whatever the fuck else to his drink. Plying him until even his bear couldn't metabolise the alcohol anymore. 'For the good of the tribe' went clean out the window once he started catering to her every whim, giving her everything she asked for. All he got in return was you. A sorry excuse of a bear. There's no alpha in you. You are not capable of ruling the tribe and returning the Torben name to its former glory among shifters."

Rygard shook his head, hefting the axe onto his shoulder again. "I know who you are. You're the exiled. Those sent away for causing endless trouble within the tribe."

"Your mother is the who caused the trouble. She pushed us out, manipulated your father into punishing our families, stripping them of their homes, businesses, and assets, all because we refused to integrate with the humans, didn't want to send our kids to the human school and close the shifter school. Those she considered the loudest agitators. We were the ones banished to appease your mother."

Rygard shook his head. "You've been gone, what? Ten years? Why come back now?"

"Because the alpha has lost his mind, and that bitch is selling out the tribe to humans."

Cord snorted, sucked on the last of his cigar before he flicked the smouldering stub into the lawn. "She has already signed the contracts. The tribe has lost over ninety percent of its assets. If you wanted to challenge the alpha to take control of the Torben tribe, you're too late."

Stevie's blood boiled when she saw Rygard's ashen face.

"And who the fuck are you?" The foot pressing her down lifted slightly.

Seizing her chance to escape, Stevie levered herself onto her hands and knees, and rolling out from under the foot. She launched to her feet and ran towards the garden gate.

"Run, baby."

Rygard's voice floated after her.

"Oh no you don't, you little slut."

Pain exploded across Stevie's scalp as she was jerked back off her feet, a meaty fist fastened around her ponytail.

"I'm not finished with you."

Tears burned at the corner of her eyes, and anger coiled in her belly. With one hand she tried to release the pressure on her scalp, while the other scratched and clawed at the hand embedded in her hair. "Let go of me, asshat," she screeched.

Foul breath washed over her face along with drops of spit, a hot head hovering at the edge of her blurred vision. "I'm going to teach you some manners."

The raucous sound of a brawl erupted behind her.

A sinewy arm anchored her to the man pinning her fast. Her feet kicked uselessly in the air.

Stevie screamed and cursed. Never had she hated her petite stature as much as she did right now.

The din diminished as her captor marched away from Rygard's home. Clouds slid across the moon, shutting off the light as the monster carried her into the seclusion of the forest.

CHAPTER NINE

CORD BUFFETT — OREGON

N othing was going to plan. Well, not everything anyway. He'd reeled Magda in hook, line, and sinker. She was greedy. Money? Power? Sex? It was all the same to her. If she thought Cord had invited her back to his cabin for more than her signature transferring the titles of the Torben properties and businesses to him, that wasn't his fault.

He'd ushered her out before the ink was dry, then returned to the bar to collect Rygard. With the rest of the logging crew already calling it a night, Rygard was happy enough to leave, driving the pair of them to his own home on the edge of the forest.

Even with Stevie's caution that BearHeart Logging was everything to Rygard, Cord did not expect the level of resistance to his proposition. It wasn't a wise move to annoy the other bear-shifter about his mother, but Cord was fighting to keep his own bear at bay.

The stubborn creature wanted Stevie and was bored of business deals. He sensed her; knew the moment she walked up the street to Rygard's home and was the reason Cord antagonised Rygard. Jealous because Stevie was coming to the other male, the hint of arousal complimenting her own sweet scent.

Years of practise at hiding his bear was all that stopped him from shifting the moment Stevie screamed, the intruder hauling the infuriatingly alluring woman into Rygard's yard. He forced himself to mask his reaction by puffing more cigar smoke into Rygard's face. The flavour was acrid in his mouth. He didn't enjoy cigars, but the smoke was a distraction, a tactic to put his opponents on the back foot, diverting the focus, even momentarily, from whatever words Cord chose to utter. He never indulged for pleasure, although did occasionally smoke when stressed beyond his control.

Magda's son — there was no way Cord considered Rygard his half-brother — released Cord's shirt. His attention redirected to the more immediate threat. Stevie being held hostage by a villainous, heavy-set bear-shifter.

Stevie was a fighter and, despite her diminutive size, grappled with the behemoth of a man holding her in the air. When she tumbled to the ground, Cord started forward, only to deflect his gesture, so it looked as though he was simply stretching to tap his cigar ash.

He let the scene play out while he rolled up his shirt sleeves, just in case, and allowed Rygard to confront the other man, begrudgingly impressed by how well the younger man held his own. Cord hadn't expected word of his corporate takeover of the Torben tribe to have spread among shifters so quickly. He anticipated having at least a week to finalise business and get the hell out of Dodge, leaving the tribe to pick up the pieces or burn under the anger of rival shifters.

It was curious that the exiled Torben bears remained in such close contact with the tribe, they already knew of and had arrived to challenge the takeover, so quickly. Hearing the other man spew his hatred for Magda, to hear him echo Muldoon's opinions of what had happened in the last twenty-eight plus years since his mother was last here — a revelation.

Cord quashed the niggle pestering his subconscious, that perhaps the tribe themselves were not to blame for his mother's fear, her trauma. That the fault lay with one woman and that she alone should be made to pay.

Finishing his cigar, Cord pondered his next move, focussing on the foul-mouthed leader of the intruders.

"Because the alpha has lost his mind, and that bitch is selling out the tribe to humans."

Cord ground the butt of his cigar into the ashtray Rygard had provided. Now was as good a time as any to step in. "She has already signed the contracts. The tribe has lost over ninety percent of its assets. If you wanted to challenge the alpha to take control of the Torben tribe, you're too late."

The ugly looking male stabbed a finger at Cord. "And who the fuck are you?"

Stevie bucked off the ground, dislodging the man who had her pinned.

She launched herself onto her feet, hearing Rygard yell, "Run, baby."

The brute recovered his balance. He spun on his heel, threading his fingers through Stevie's ponytail and yanked her upright before she could flee the danger.

Rygard spun into action, he wielded his axe left and right. His muscles moved smoothly, rippling with the action of a well-practised swing. Cord could visualise him, in the forest, felling trees with deadly accuracy. Instead, he chopped down at least one shifter. The man's agonised screams rent the air, fuelling the blood lust of Cord's bear.

Cord ignored the melee in Rygard's yard, and jumped from the deck to the grass, skirting the free-for-all against the younger bear. He would either be the victor, or he wouldn't. Cord didn't care. His objective was Stevie and the man who hauled her away into the forest. She was *his*.

Cord's legs buckled as the vehemence of his bear's intention nearly knocked him on his ass. Stevie wasn't his. She was a means to an end. Taking her from Rygard would be the icing on the cake in destroying Magda and her family for what she had put his mother through. The woman went to her grave in fear of shifters because of some complete and utter bullshit concocted by a jealous hag who wanted a man never meant to be hers.

The clouds drifted over the three-quarter full moon, plunging the land into darkness and his target vanished into the forest.

Cord growled, "Shit."

He was walking blind without moonlight to guide him. He stopped, closed his eyes, and drew in a deep breath. He concentrated on leashing the feral nature of his bear then allowed the beast enough prominence that his eyes shifted, providing a greater depth of vision in the obscurity. With a confident stride, he headed for the tree line.

Cord grinned. With bark scuffed off several trees to his right, he was able to follow the distinct trail left by Stevie's duel with her captor. He could almost visualise the little spitfire digging her heels into every log, branch, and trunk she could reach to make the trek that little bit harder for the bastard dragging her off to who knew where.

Before long he heard the muffled sounds of bickering. His little hellcat was giving her assailant no quarter, Cord was sure that her kidnapper would die from a thousand verbal cuts if he didn't get there soon enough and pummel his own brand of punishment into the bastard.

"Stop kicking, you little bitch."

"Then let me go, creep."

"Not until I've taught you a lesson, you and that witch's whelp."

Stevie yelped. "Touch me, you fucker, and I'll rip your dick off and shove it so far up your ass you'll be spitting it out."

Cord smothered a guffaw, he wasn't sure what the guy had done but, given her threat, he could imagine.

"Ha, I'd like to see you try."

Cord slowed his pace, the outline of bodies, clear to his enhanced sight. Stevie was tossed to the ground, the great brute following her down until he was straddling her hips.

Clenching his jaw as he battled to control his beast, Cord entered the fray. "Why don't you pick on someone your own size?"

The guy looked over his shoulder, one eyebrow arched as he spotted Cord. "Well, if it isn't Mr Pretty Boy. You might be more my own size, but you're not my type." His hand tightened around Stevie's jaw. "This is the sort of mouth I'd rather use."

Stevie tried to spit at him, but with the grip of his hand around her face, it caught on her lip and dribbled down her jaw.

"Save it for my cock, princess," he jibed. "I just have to deal with the fru-fru then you're all mine." His fist clipped the corner of Stevie's face.

When Cord saw her head loll to one side, her eyes flutter closed, he thundered, "You'll pay for touching her, you bastard."

With Stevie subdued, the other male got to his feet. He spun around to face Cord.

Fists flew.

Left, left, right, left, right, right, left.

Cord jabbed with the full force of his anger and strength. Blood splattered across his knuckles when the nose his fist connected with exploded.

His opponent stumbled backwards and shook his head, spraying droplets in an arc. He tore his shirt over his head, his growl deepened, becoming more animalistic with the rapid shift from man to beast.

Cord's left hand faltered, dropping below his chin, and his eyes widened as a shaggy looking grizzly replaced the man.

Wicked, yellow teeth snapped. The furry muzzle skimmed Cord's head, the hot breath chuffing into his face held the rancid odour of a poor diet.

Cord's knuckles cracked as he delivered a right hook to the wet nose.

Dazed, the bear wobbled on his hind legs then dropped onto all fours.

Cord removed his shirt, toed off his shoes and shrugged out of his dress pants, barely avoiding the swipe of a giant paw as the grizzly swatted at him. He let the shift race through him, reshaping his form, and covering him with the thick fur of his Kodiak bear.

The grizzly rocked back onto his hind feet then propelled himself forward.

Claws and teeth clashed, locking in a vicious embrace as the two bears tumbled to the ground.

Pain sliced through Cord's side, claws scraping his rib bones. He roared, and let his bear have more control, trusting the beast possessed the raw instinct to fight another bear. This was certainly nothing like the pugilism of boxing. Blood bubbled around his teeth currently buried deep in the shoulder of his adversary.

The claws withdrew from his side as a bellow of pain reverberated in his sensitive ears. Ripping his jaws out, Cord released the other bear, spitting fur and flesh to the forest floor as the two beasts separated.

At that moment, the clouds parted, bathing the clearing in moonlight.

Stevie groaned, drawing her abductor's attention. His beady eyes gleamed and, instead of charging Cord again, the grizzly bounded towards the tiny female.

Cord roared, every ounce of his dominance flooded the glade, ricocheting off the trees, the sheer power of the lone alpha bowled over the other male. Cord catapulted himself across the space in three steps and, seizing the creature's neck in his great paws, squeezed.

The grizzly whined, and the fight left him. His body sagged under Cord's grip, and he shifted. "I submit," he wheezed, eyeing the fiendishly sharp claws of the alpha, latched around his throat.

Bloodlust blazed through Cord, fuelling the beast's rage. His claws didn't tighten, but neither did he release his foe. Sickened, Cord fought to regain control.

A small hand speared into his fur, cold, gentle fingers sizzled against his fevered skin.

"Cord. He has submitted. You can let him go."

The Kodiak swung his head towards the soft voice. Bright, cat-like eyes stared up at him, and rosettes ghosted across an otherwise perfect skin. Cord blinked. He had never witnessed another shifter suppressing a transition to their beast before.

Static zapped along his paw, emanating from a delicate finger drawing circles on his skin beneath the thick layer of fur.

"Yeah man, I submitted. Let me go."

Cord rumbled again, his head swinging back towards the man frozen in his grasp.

"Shut up, asshole." Stevie kicked his shin. "I'm trying to placate the beast and you're trying to rile the bugger up again. Keep it up, genius and I'll let him chomp your motherfucking head off."

The magnitude of the woman's mettle, dwarfed Cord's bear. Her compassionate touch, compared with her attitude had his bear rumbling a deep belly laugh. The Kodiak's control slackened, and Cord came into ascendency. Strengthening his mental reins, he slammed the door shut on his beast. The night air was chill against his naked skin, the reversal faster than his earlier shift.

Cord's hand remained clamped around the neck of his opponent. He coerced his gaze away from Stevie, to focus on the cringing oaf in his clutches. "Apologise to the lady now, or I'll let the beast out to snack on you."

His throat worked under Cord's hand. "I...I...I'm s...s...sorry."

Cord's lip curled in disgust, and he glared at the back of the other man's head. "Piss off. Now." Cord relinquished his grip with an emphatic shove, and the defeated male staggered forward. Cord watched him stoop to gather his clothes before he bolted. Only when he had vanished from sight, did Cord look at Stevie.

The rosettes of her inner cat had faded away, instead two high spots of red stained her face, highlighting her cheekbones. "I..." She swallowed. "I always thought you were a bear of a man."

Enfolding Stevie in his arms, Cord chuckled. "And you told me not to call you kitten."

Her head tipped back, her eyes on his. "What?"

Cord's thumb brushed her chin; his touch, featherlight, skimmed over her skin to the bruise blossoming at the corner of her eye. "I saw the eyes and the hint of rosettes peppering your skin. You're a big cat shifter."

Startled, her perfect mouth formed a silent 'oh'. She dipped her head, then met his inquisitive gaze again. "Arabian leopard," she confessed.

"Pretty." He grinned.

She smothered a smile. "Yeah."

He lowered his head, grazed his nose along hers, their breath mingling. His lips hovered over hers, teasing her with the promise of a kiss.

Slender fingers circled his arm, the tips pressing into his muscle.

With a grin, Cord moved closer, hungering to taste her.

A bear roared. Branches crashed and timber cracked. The ground trembled with the heavy thud of something large and angry bounding towards them.

Cord manoeuvred Stevie until she was behind him, hidden and protected, as an immense Kodiak burst into the clearing.

CHAPTER TEN

STEVIE RAHAL — OREGON

Stevie knew an alpha when she saw one. Her cat had responded instantly to the superior authority, Cord exuded fighting the Torben exile. Stevie had been cursing her feline for not letting her shift to fight the man threatening to assault her.

Until Cord arrived. She understood her leopard's behaviour then. The creature knew he was coming and waited for the alpha. *Her* alpha.

The ferocity of the manic beast stomping towards them was off the charts. Stevie's chest constricted, even from behind Cord's back — a delightful back, and one she would love to explore, just not while they were about to be eaten — she recognised the unstable strength of the Torben alpha.

Her hand settled on the tight curve of Cord's ass. The contact grounded her, fizzing up her like the spasm caused by an electric fence. Her heart drummed in her chest, her mouth watered and, by way his skin quivered under her touch, he was affected equally.

"Cord," she hissed. "That's the alpha, that's Rygard's dad. He's dangerous, Cord, you can't reason with him."

Cord angled his head to catch her eye. "I need you to shift, kitten. You'll be faster, and stronger. Can you do that? Can you shift?"

"Of course, I can shift," she retorted.

"Well, you haven't yet, so—" he shrugged a shoulder, the bulging muscle flexing. "—I wasn't sure if you, you know, could."

Stevie poked Cord's butt, her finger barely dented the taut flesh. "I thought I'd hang around to see if I'd get rescued first."

The enraged Kodiak paced; savage fangs bared in menacing challenge.

Cord stiffened. "Don't sass me now, Stevie. I need you to shift and get your tush out of here. Immediately."

Energy coiled around her, sinking into her flesh. Her cat purred, and Stevie nearly came in response to Cord's dominance. Shaken, Stevie whipped off her kaftan, the material fluttering onto Cord's clothing while she discarded her pants.

The magic of her own shift began in her chest, streaking through her, the way lightening sliced the sky during a storm. Her body contorted, bones breaking and reforming until with a yowl, she landed on cushioned paws in the leaf litter of the forest. Her tail swished, slapping Cord's calf muscle and winding around his leg.

Stevie mewled, enticing her alpha with the caress of her silky fur. She hated to leave him. Something within her demanded she stay at his side, but Cord had given her an order, and her cat couldn't, wouldn't disobey. He had claimed her loyalty without even trying.

Growling low in her throat, Stevie sprang away from Cord and the approaching bear. Spotting a low hanging branch, she leapt up, her claws digging into the bark, giving her enough purchase to climb the tree and find a perch on a thick branch. Head on the limb, she squinted through the leaves to watch Cord.

The wound from the dipshit's claws had stopped bleeding, and the raw, ugly looking mess knitted together in front of Stevie's eyes. Cord's shift undulated along his body, with the speed of a racing wave, the Herculean man transforming into a gargantuan bear once more.

Flattening his ears, Cord grunted, and dropped to all fours, charging at the advancing bear. His teeth clacked, and his breath huffed out in a noisy display of dominance.

Stevie whined. Finally, she had found a male to whom she would gladly surrender, and he was stupid enough to provoke a shifter gone mad, subsumed by his animal. All before he could show her exactly what an alpha male could do to a bratty female. *Why did Cord have to challenge the alpha?* Her claws flexed, burrowing into the green wood, then retracting. Her stiffened tail flicked back and forth, displaying her agitation.

The older Kodiak moved into her field of vision. His body language mirrored Cord's. The pair circled each other, heads jutting forward as they gnashed their teeth threateningly.

From Stevie's bird's eye view, their sinuous movements were reminiscent of the yin and yang symbol. Streaks of grey, in the matted fur of the older bear, the only distinction between the two colossal animals.

The older bear sized up his younger opponent and dropped to his haunches.

Cord paused, one ear pricked up. Stevie could almost hear the cogs of his mind grinding at the unexpected behaviour of the deranged bear.

Power flowed across the forest, prickling Stevie's body like an army of ants on the march. She froze, unable to blink at the scene unfolding in front of her.

Ryan Jones, alpha of the Torben pack sat in front of Cord. Human. Naked as a newborn baby for the first time in almost three years. His mouth worked, opening, and closing several times until he finally uttered one word. "Lizzie?"

Cord swung his big brown head in her direction, his deep, dark, bottomless eyes bored into her soul.

Stevie knew. It resonated in her soul. Her alpha needed her.

She levered herself off the wood but didn't stand completely upright. Her centre of gravity low, she crept backwards until she reached the main trunk of the sprawling white oak. Manoeuvring her body, so she could climb down the tree headfirst.

When Stevie reached her pile of clothes, her nose crinkled at the distinctive scent of salt. Peering at Rygard's father, she was surprised to find tears washing down his face.

Whiskers twitching, Stevie lowered her head to grab her kaftan. Gingerly, she picked it up, careful not to puncture the silk with her teeth. Ducking behind a tree for cover, she closed her eyes. It took more concentration than usual to shift back, her skin pebbling with gooseflesh the instant the cold night air enveloped her two-legged form.

Clothed, she padded quietly through the leaf litter to reach Cord. It was the first time she had seen Rygard's father as a human. She had spotted him a few times over the years as a bear, ambling through the forest, or even right up the main street of town.

Stevie reached Cord, her fingers gliding into his fur as she tried to clasp one of his humongous mitts, an impossible feat, given his paw was bigger than her torso, and his claws as long as her forearm. He was deadly, one swipe could eviscerate her, but she wasn't afraid. For all he emitted dangerous vibes in his human form, from his dark, broody looks to his nasty cigar puffing habits, he was nothing more than an enormous teddy bear she could sink into.

Cord dropped to his haunches, mimicking Ryan's posture before he shifted. Only Cord didn't shift. He stayed as a bear.

The night air was getting colder. Shivering, Stevie climbed onto Cord's lap, wriggling to make herself comfortable, her back against his abdomen.

He looped an arm around her, safeguarding her and creating a luxurious cocoon of thick fur. He rumbled, the sound thrumming through her body straight to her core.

Rather than wallow in the pleasure of using the bear as a giant vibrating seat, she scrutinised Rygard's father who in turn, hands in his lap to maintain some form of modesty, contemplated her.

His body was larger than Rygard's. Bulkier, with more mass. Had she not seen photos from Rygard's childhood, she might question whether Ryan was still channelling his bear after three years as the animal. In truth he had always been a big human. Like Cord.

Stevie scanned the alpha's wet cheeks. His tears had stopped flowing, but pain remained etched across his features. He swallowed, his Adam's apple bobbing in his throat. His head lolled, his bushy beard brushing his defined pectorals. White and grey dominated his facial hair and fanned out in streaks over his head from his temple, aging the alpha, giving him the haggard countenance of a shifter at the end of his life, rather than a man who should be in his prime.

"Don't ever let anyone come between you," he rasped.

Stevie frowned. "Excuse me?"

"True mates. True power. Sanity. Should never be parted."

"What? I don't know what you're saying."

The fur of Cord's bear slid across her skin, tickling as it receded with his shift. Stevie hardly felt the monstrous bear shrink into the enormous man. His skin radiated heat, his arm around her midriff, his manhood erect under her ass.

Stevie tingled, her core ached, her pussy clenched.

Cord rubbed his bristled jaw on the top of her head. "I know what he is saying."

"Lizzie's boy?" Ryan's voice cracked. His eyes misted. "My boy?"

Cord's nod was nearly lost in Stevie's hair. A droplet landed on her ear, trickling down to her lobe.

"Yes," Cord breathed. "My mother was your true mate, Magda used vile words to poison her against you, send her running for safety. She spent her life terrified of shifters, tormented by nightmares, screaming as they hunted her in her dreams."

Stevie pressed trembling fingers to her lips, and her eyes burned with the effort not to weep. "Cord, you said *was*."

He nodded. "She died almost three years ago."

Ryan flinched, and tears spilled over his cheeks. "When my bear snapped."

"Magda may have drugged you enough to ensnare you, captured your attention enough to remove your focus from all other women, but she couldn't sever the connection which exists between true mates. She had to get rid of my mother before you broke free of her spell and had to trick you into claiming her as your mate, but she couldn't trap you forever."

Ryan scrubbed at his face, folded his legs up to his chest, and dropped his head onto his knees. "For the first time in years I can see with clarity." He gave a nose rattling sniff. "It's like watching an old video recording, I don't remember it, but I see it. Every time she spiked my drinks with caraway, an aphrodisiac designed to cloud my judgement, everything felt so good, how could she not be my mate? My bear knew. He knew, but I silenced him. Magda's perfume, he hated it, would retreat from my consciousness rather than deal with it. Me, the man... I loved it, it smelled sublime, and she was a stunner. God, I wanted her."

Cord sighed. "Muldoon called her a witch."

Stevie interjected, "Witches aren't real. There's no such thing as magic among humans, even shifters only have the ability to shift."

Ryan barked out a harsh laugh. "Oh, she's a witch, alright. Admitted as much herself when I first met her, just without the moniker. She's always cultivated plants, herbs, spices, and flowers. Made a living from it. After all, plants are inherently valuable, they are the basis of most healing remedies. Even crystals and rocks can possess natural earth energy which can be used by humans and shifters alike."

Stevie felt Cord stroke his fingers along her side. The sensation rocked her, and it took all she had to corral her wayward brain back to the matter at hand, to hear him say, "California is full of new age, hippy-dippy people. They use aromatherapy for everything. It can promote healing, repel insects, encourage sleep—"

The older bear snorted. "Attract alpha bears."

Cord dipped his head, his stubble snagging in her hair. "I was going to say stimulate sexual attraction."

"Hang on a cotton-pickin' minute." Stevie clutched Cord's forearm and twisted to face him. "*You're* the alpha's true heir to Torben?"

Cord scowled, and his face darkened. "No."

"No," echoed Ryan. "He is *already* the alpha of the Torben tribe. I submitted to his challenge."

Cord's chest inflated, and his body expanded around Stevie. "I didn't challenge you. I don't want the tribe."

"Then why buy it all?" Stevie countered.

Ryan stabbed a finger at Cord, his reply drowning out Stevie's question. "Yes, you did. The moment you sent your mate away and shifted, you challenged me. Are you so ignorant of your heritage, you have no idea what you did when you charged at me?"

The hand on Stevie's waist tightened, as Cord fought for control of his anger. "I was raised by humans in the human world. I understand everything there is to know about the corporate world. I can cut down any business rival, wipe the boardroom floor with him and not even need to take off my jacket to do it." He flung a hand towards Ryan, then spread his arm to encompass the forest. "This? Here? Is a foreign world to me."

Laughter boomed out of Ryan. "You are a natural born leader, my boy—"

"I'm not your boy," interrupted Cord.

Ryan continued as though Cord hadn't spoken, "—your bear has all the instincts he needs. You possess the innate instincts of an alpha. It's what attracted me to you. You wielded your power, dominated a hostile bear. The area reeks of the fight, so don't deny it."

"He was going to hurt, Stevie. I couldn't let that happen." Cord ducked his head, his cheek brushing Stevie's, the pressure of his fingers on her ribs increased.

Stevie nuzzled Cord's forearm. "You exude it even when you try to hide it, Cord. It's why Rygard got all clingy. He sensed your supremacy but didn't understand it. You are alpha. You are the future of Pineville, of the Torben tribe."

"No." Cord stood up. He held Stevie long enough for her to find her feet, then spun on his heel and strode over to where his suit pants and shirt lay in a crumpled heap on the dirt. He dragged on his pants, and flung his shirt over his shoulder, the dirty white material hung off his finger, flapping behind him as he stalked out of the glade.

Rooted to the spot, Stevie watched him disappear into the darkness, then looked down at Ryan Jones. "What the hell just happened?"

"Too much for either of us to comprehend, child," murmured the old alpha. "Come on, let's get back to town," he added and shifted back into his bear.

CHAPTER ELEVEN

CORD BUFFETT — OREGON

Rygard was limping when Cord came across him at the edge of the forest, several other Torben shifters with him.

Cord sniffed, looking down his nose at the younger male. "You survived then?"

Rygard batted away the question with one of his own. "Where's Stevie?"

With a jerk of his head over his shoulder, Cord gave the young man what he wanted. "I left her with your father."

Wide-eyed, Rygard snared Cord's arm, arresting his stride. "Are you freaking crazy? Dad's a mindless bear. She's not safe with him. No one is."

Cord snarled and stepped into Rygard's personal space. Towering over the other male, he spoke through gritted teeth. "I wouldn't leave her in danger, you little shit. Your father is fine, and so is Stevie, now take your fucking hand off me, before I rip it from your arm and beat you with it."

Rygard shoved Cord's arm into him. "Whatever, asshole," he stomped off in the direction Cord had just come. He didn't get far when he spun around. "You know, everything was just fine until you showed up. Now, everything's gone to shit. I think it's time you crawled back under whatever rock you slithered out from."

With a mirthless laugh, Cord flipped Rygard the bird and resumed his march to the road. "Get used to it, pup, I'm not going anywhere," he called over his shoulder.

"If I didn't have to rescue Stevie from my dad, I'd hand you your ass on a platter," Rygard scoffed, limping further into the forest. "If she's hurt, I swear, I'll hunt you down and kill you."

Cord's bear slammed against his mental walls, prepared to tear the head off the insolent whelp. Cord gnashed his teeth so hard, he was sure he had ground off a crown or two from his molars. He lengthened his stride, determined to put some distance between them and not lose supremacy. Now was *not* the time to snap.

"Pussy," The insult was sneered.

It struck Cord like a dead weight, and that was all it took. With a menacing growl he flung down his soiled shirt and stormed after Rygard's retreating form.

He yanked the hickory wood handle of the axe from the younger bear's grasp, spinning him around in the process. "You might hold your own against a couple of punk ass thugs when you've got an axe in hand, you little shit, but let's see how you fare in a bare knuckle against an alpha."

Rygard gaped at Cord. It took him a moment to recover. "I don't have time for this bullshit. Give me back my axe, I need to find Stevie."

Cord hefted the axe and pitched it at the nearest tree. It spun, end over end, skimming past the head of another shifter who ducked just in time, to lodge deep in the rough bark of an ancient tree. "I told you, she's fine."

A handful of the younger shifters with Rygard, sprinted towards the pair.

Cord faced them; his hand cut through the air; he pointed at the closest. "Stay put," he ordered; the words resounded with alpha power across the small clearing.

Everyone stopped in their tracks. Eyes like saucers, they struggled to comprehend the force buffeting them.

"How?"

Rygard had scarcely formed the question when Cord tapped him with a left hook.

Rygard's fingers curled into fists, and he swung a couple of bar room punches at the larger man.

Cord dodged them with ease. Elbows tucked in, he shaped up, fists hovering in front of his face and, balancing on the balls of his feet, one foot in front of the other, he countered his opponent.

Rygard ducked and weaved. He didn't move with the same grace and style as Cord, but he had obviously held his own in an occasional brawl. Aiming for Cord's throat, Rygard's fist glanced off the older man's elbow. Stepping sideways, into Cord's sphere, Rygard travelled past and, jerking his arm back, drove his elbow in the tender spot above Cord's kidney.

Cord stumbled, stifling the expletive, refusing to give Rygard have the satisfaction of knowing he had landed a sound blow. He pivoted on his heel to face the younger man and, ignoring all the rules and etiquette of the pugilist, throwing himself into an all-out brawl. Cord rushed his opponent; trying to hook one arm around Rygard's neck, while pummelling Rygard's back with the other.

Rygard surprised Cord. He held his own, landing plenty of well-placed punches across the tender flesh of the recently healed wound from his earlier scuffle.

Rygard weaselled his way out of Cord's clutches, and head butted him in the throat, accompanied by a swift jab to Cord's ribs.

Angered, Cord kicked the bloodied section of Rygard's lower leg.

The younger man crumpled onto one knee, yelping in pain.

Cord followed with a sharp right hook, ready to knock him out cold.

A small hand grabbed the crook of his elbow, thwarting his attack. A familiar voice exhorted. "Enough."

He wrenched his eyes from Rygard, to meet the cat-like gaze of Stevie.

Rygard aimed a fist at Cord's groin.

Stevie lifted her leg, deflecting his blow with her bare foot. "I said, that's enough, Paddington Bear."

Cord spat out a glob of blood and sniggered at Stevie's use of the children's favourite cuddly bear name for Rygard.

Stevie glared at Cord, putting a halt to his amusement.

"Babe," Rygard appealed.

"Don't you babe me." Stevie prodded her finger into Rygard's bloodied nose. She slapped his hand away when he ran it up the back of her thigh. "I told you, we're just having a bit of fun."

Hearing Cord's snort, Stevie rounded on him. "How dare you walk away from me..." she punctuated each word with a sharp poke to several blossoming bruises across his middle, "...when there is so much to discuss. When you're..."

Abruptly, Cord caught her ponytail and tugged her to his chest. She angled away from him, but he held her fast, cutting off her tirade with a finger to her lips. "Not. Now. Kitten."

She bit his finger and glared at him.

"Not. Now." Cord repeated, his nose flaring as he quashed his bear's desire to sink into her in front of everyone.

Nervous whispers rippled across the clearing, followed by the unmistakeable stirring in the atmosphere, indicative of an alpha shifting.

Cord recognised Ryan's presence but ignored him, his eyes pinned on Stevie.

"Let her go, Cord." Ryan's voice vibrated with his deep, raspy rumble.

"Why?" he retaliated, one brow raised as he continued to scowl at Stevie. "The brat needs to know when to keep her mouth shut."

Ryan gave a rusty laugh, and clapped his hand on Cord's shoulder. "Keep that for behind closed doors, boy."

"Dad?" Rygard fell on his ass; twisting to keep his father in his sights.

Rygard's shocked question broke through the haze of lust that swamped Cord when the rush of Stevie's instant arousal smacked him in the olfactory centre.

Cord smirked at Stevie. He slipped his finger past her lips, skimmed across her teeth, teased her tongue for a moment, and withdrew it, tweaking her lower lip as he did. "Later," he promised with a wink.

Colour bloomed over her cheeks, and her chest heaved.

With obvious reluctance, Cord released Stevie's hair. Her hand slid over his abdominal muscles, settling in the waistband of his slacks as she steadied herself.

Ryan ignored his younger son and behaved as though the other males weren't present. He padded across to the puddle of white on the ground. "Whose shirt is this?" He lifted it to his nose. "Ah. Cord's. I'm borrowing it."

Cord suppressed an angry retort when the older male tied the expensive shirt around his hips to cover his modesty.

Rygard struggled to his feet and surged to his father. "Dad, you're okay?"

"I'm...I guess I'm better than I was." Ryan cupped one hand around his son's face, the other engulfed his shoulder.

Cord snorted. "I told you he was fine, and that Stevie was safe." His voice fading, he muttered, "insolent little brat thinking he knows better than me."

Stevie heard him and pressed a finger on a nasty looking bruise near his navel.

With a growl, Cord snared her ponytail and give it a quick jerk, chastising her with his eyes. Her unrepentant smile, along with the gleam in her eyes told him she would be a handful to deal with once he got her in his bed. His bear relished the chance to claim her, to curb her sass without crushing her wild spirit.

"What happened to you? Mom couldn't call you back to us. Your bear wouldn't let you shift," Rygard whispered.

Ryan regarded the other shifters, standing where Cord had told them to stay. "Go home, let me speak with my son in private."

No one moved.

Eyes rolling, Cord commanded, in tones that brooked no argument, "You heard the man. Get lost. Now."

Shocked looks were shared, but they complied. In one group they trooped out of the forest and drifted away. Only the Jones's, Cord and Stevie were left.

Stunned, Rygard gaped at the two men. "What?" he stabbed a finger at Cord. "You. What did you do? Why is everyone obeying you? What the fuck are you doing in Pineville? Why has everything gone wrong since you showed up?"

Cord folded his arms, holding them a little higher to clear the top of Stevie's head. "*I* didn't bring those exiled punks to town."

Rygard's chin jutted forward. "No? They mention the tribe being sold off. You're the corporate ass flapping your gums about buying BearHeart Logging. You even said the contracts had been signed and that ninety percent of the tribe's assets are now sold. How are you *not* responsible for those punks being in town?"

"Rygard," Ryan reached out to press a hand on Rygard's shoulder. "Calm down."

The younger man shrugged his father away, his eyes glinting, "Don't think you can gallivant about as a bear for three damn years, abandoning not only the tribe, but me and mom, then just rock up like nothing's changed, telling me to calm down."

"Ry," Stevie murmured. "No one can tell you anything if you don't listen."

His gaze seared her. His face darkened as he registered how close to Cord, she was standing. "Just a bit of fun hey, Stevie? So, you can jump into bed with the next shifter who catches your eye without worrying about breaking anyone's trust?"

"Trust?" hissed Stevie, she advanced on Rygard, finger jabbing his chest. "Trust? You want to talk to me about breaking someone's trust? You pushed past the explicit boundaries I set. I knew we weren't mates. *You* knew we weren't mates. It was a casual fling while we waited for either one of us to find our mate or we drifted apart. You're the one who started with the public displays of affection at work and pushing for something more."

Rygard snatched Stevie's wrist and hauled her up against him. "Who said you're not mine?"

"Ry?" Stevie struggled to speak, her voice stuck in her throat, eyes fixed on Rygard's curled upper lip, and his lengthening canines.

The younger shifter moved so fast; Cord did not realise his intent.

In a split second, Rygard had lifted Stevie off the ground, one arm clamped her to his torso, the other wound around her ponytail, angling her head. His face nuzzled the crook of her neck.

The scent of her blood blossomed on the night air.

Her scream rent the clearing.

CHAPTER TWELVE

STEVIE RAHAL — OREGON

Ice turned to fire as pain lanced through her neck and shoulder. The coppery tang of blood filled the air, its warm wetness oozing over tender skin. Her cat hissed within her, paws battering at her mental walls wanting to rip into Rygard for daring to sink his teeth into her body.

Her fingers curled against his chest, claws unsheathed, scratching through the thin tee stretched over his body. Black crowded her vision, and she blinked rapidly in an effort clear it. Hanging in Rygard's grasp, she kicked him repeatedly, but her onslaught was weakening.

Gentle hands came around her waist, taking her weight, and cradling her against a strong body.

Rygard's teeth tore from her flesh, blood splashing into her shoulder.

Her eyelids flickered and she caught sight of Cord behind Rygard, face shuttered in a scowl, the latter's hair clenched in an iron hand. Blood dripped from Rygard's teeth, staining his face scarlet.

Everything went black, and she was unaware of being lowered, carefully, to the ground. The moment passed and as Stevie regained consciousness, she was relieved to feel the spears of pain in her neck began to withdraw, ebbing to a dull ache. The thunderous cacophony of her pulse in her ears faded allowing Cord's words to reach her.

"You fucking idiot."

She realised that Ryan was kneeling behind her, propping her upright while he fussed at her wound.

Forcing her eyes open, Stevie focused on Cord who had Rygard's shirt in his fist. The younger shifter's toes brushed the leaf litter as Cord hauled him up until they were face to face.

"Did you really think you could claim Stevie in front of me and that it would *work*? I wasn't raised in a tribe like you but even I know mate marks don't work like that."

Stevie's back quivered with Ryan's grumbled interjection.

"I expected better from you, boy." There was a chuff of hot breath against her neck. "I guess you are more like your mother than I'd like to admit."

Rygard kicked at Cord's knee, and thumped Cord's upper arms, to no discernible effect. "Put me down, asshole. It's just a bit of fun..." he twisted to look over at Stevie, "...right, babe?"

Her eyebrows furrowed. "Just a bit of fun? *Fun*?" Stevie hissed, her cat echoing within her mind. She inched out from under Ryan's protective hands, using him as a lever to stand.

Her first couple of steps were shaky, but by the time she reached Cord and Rygard, she had found her strength.

Her childhood, spent scrapping with her brothers, had taught her a thing or two about holding her own. "Fuck you, Paddington Bear." She took aim and her foot made a solid connection with Rygard's crotch.

"This..." she pulled down her stained kaftan, revealing more of her mauled shoulder, "...is not 'a bit of fun'. I should've let Cord beat you to a pulp earlier, then maybe I wouldn't have this supersized flea bite."

Cord released Rygard who crumpled to the ground.

Rygard groaned, rolling into a foetal position until he could nurse his injured manhood.

Stevie peered down her nose, wrinkled in disgust, at Rygard. "Find yourself another logger. I quit." She wheeled around and flounced off.

Her steps were matched by a heavy tread. She glanced over her shoulder, wincing when her swiftly-healing wound twinged. She spied Cord following her, and with a resigned huff, stopped and waited from him to catch up. She wobbled on her feet and her vision dimmed momentarily.

Cord came alongside and placed one large hand on her lower back, the other hooked around her arm, steadying her on her feet.

"Are you okay?"

A frisson ran through her at his tender touch. She shrugged him off before her cat carried her away with wild ideas of plastering herself to his body and never letting go. "Yeah, I'm fine, well, I will be anyway. I just need a bath and to get out of these clothes."

"May I walk you home? Make sure you get there in one piece." He gave a troubled laugh. "You know what they say about everything happening in threes."

Too tired to argue, Stevie smiled wearily, looking at him from the corner of her eye. "That's a load of phooey in my humble opinion."

His step faltered.

She faced him. His eyes gleamed with his inner bear, and the air seethed with unbridled power. "But, sure. You may escort me home if it keeps your bear calm." Her formal reply softened when she held out her hand.

A ghost of a grin banished Cord's anxious frown, and he engulfed her hand with his.

A companionable silence enveloped the pair as they trudged through the forest until they reached the short cul-de-sac where Rygard lived. The tranquillity of the night belied the previous disturbance. A handful of broken branches in Rygard's hedge, the only evidence of the earlier altercation.

Tormented by images of being pinned under the foot of the exiled bear shifter, a shiver skittered down Stevie's spine.

Cord squeezed her hand. The wordless gesture brought her back to the here and now, grounding her. She reciprocated and lengthened her stride. She wanted to get back to the comfort of her own home, and surround herself with the familiar. Cord matched her pace, keeping up with her effortlessly.

Soon, Stevie detected the delicate honey-almond-vanilla fragrance of the night phlox in her garden. It settled her mind and lifted her soul. Her lips curved, and her step quickened.

"This is me," Stevie cleared her throat, her hand curled around the top of her gate. "I'm safely home."

Cord's free hand ran through his hair to settle on his nape. He scanned the brick façade of her home. "That bastard was watching you and you didn't even know it. He knows where you live. I want to scout inside, make sure you are safe. My conscience wouldn't allow me to leave without checking."

Stevie grinned. "Your conscience or your bear?"

"Honestly? I'm not sure which is which right now, or whether there is even a distinction between the two," he admitted ruefully

"There *is* a difference." She nudged his side with their joined hands, reluctant to let him go. "Trust me, I know."

Cord arched a brow. "I can count on one hand the number of people who have my trust."

"Oh—"

He tugged her closer, "There's room on that hand to include you."

She was unable to prevent the blush which stole up her pale cheeks . Swinging the gate open she pulled him through with her. "In that case, I suppose you ought to ensure my house is safe from invaders and men of nefarious intent."

She brushed past the flowers, the subtle scent intensifying with the fresh release of fragrance. She inhaled deeply, centring herself in the restorative properties of the night blooming plant.

Cord angled himself ahead of her as they reached the front door. "Where's your key?"

"It's not locked—"

The irritated growl he released cut her off. "Why do you not keep your home locked?"

She blinked at him, eyes round in disbelief. "This isn't the big city, you know. Shifters have a level of trust here in Pineville. A person can leave their home and be sure they won't be harassed by any uninvited guests."

He scoffed. "But tonight—"

"Tonight nothing," she retorted. "That was outside the realm of normal."

He pressed a finger to her mouth, halting her protests. "That might be so, kitten, but that's all the more reason I should ensure your home is safe now." He plucked her lower lip as he removed his finger.

Stevie blinked, then drew in a shaky breath when he ducked to avoid smacking his head on the lintel, the action emphasising his impressive size.

Never relinquishing her hand, he tucked her behind him, so close her nose brushed the bare skin of his back, and it was all she could do not to taste the sweat on his skin.

Instead, she followed blindly along the hallway to the kitchen, by-passing the closed door of the living room.

There wasn't much to see. Besides the typical array of appliances, a small table and two chairs were arranged against one wall, opposite a glass door led to the backyard. A security light illuminated the tiny space packed with raised planters overflowing with a multitude of fresh vegetables, the moment the door was thrown wide.

Cord gave a curt nod, closed the door and engaged the lock, then manoeuvred them both out of the kitchen, stopping at the closed door beyond. It swung open with ease when he rested his fingers on the wood panelling.

When Cord grunted, Stevie poked her head around his side, taking in the jumbled sight. In front of the sofa, the only item of soft furnishing in the space, a glass coffee table, covered with grease-stained newspapers. The one corner that was not obscured reflected the glow streaming in through the window from the exterior streetlight.

The overtones of sawdust, oil, gas, and metal filings were reminiscent of a mechanic's shop, and her Husqvarna sat in pride of place on the paper, her tools scattered around it. A small jerry can, along with bottles of two-stroke and bar oil sat in a hard plastic basket under the table.

"Nothing out of place in there," she said, trying to usher him away from the messy space, her stomach knotting at the thought he was judging her.

He looked at her, his expression unreadable. "No TV?"

Stevie shrugged, grimacing when the tender flesh of her neck stretched. "I have a laptop if I want to stream anything. A TV sitting on the side, unwatched for most of the day is a wasted expense."

Cord nodded and closed the door with a quiet click. "What's upstairs?"

"A bedroom and bathroom. Honestly, this place isn't much, but it's big enough for me, and the rent is modest."

"I'll check it's clear upstairs, although honestly I only smell you and," disdain in his tone, "Rygard. Except in there of course, it stinks like a workshop in there." He added, jerking his head towards the living room.

"I don't normally have guests," she murmured, traipsing up the stairs after him, her hand still securely in his.

Cord stooped when the angle of ceiling above the stairs tapered, scarcely avoiding a bang to the head.

Stevie grinned. He was more aware of his surroundings than Rygard. No matter how many times he had climbed the stairs, nine times out of ten he hit his head at least once on the way up or down.

Cord went straight through Stevie's bedroom, to the adjoining bathroom. He whistled when he saw the tub dominating the space. "Nice bath."

"Yeah," Stevie croaked, all her mental energy busy shutting down her randy cat's mental imagery of Cord and her in the tub. "It's why I settled on renting this place. I'm a sucker for a hot bath, day, or night."

His hand skimmed the various oil bottles lining the small shelf above the tub, and he inhaled the residual fragrances now clinging to his fingers. "You don't use just one, you blend them, right?"

Stevie blinked. "Err, yeah. I do. How'd you know?"

He rubbed his thumb and fingers together under his nose, a twinkle in his eye. "Do you want to run yourself a bath while I check under the bed and in the closet for monsters?"

She nodded numbly. Whatever ideas and opinions she had formed about Cord Buffett, initially, only one of them held true. He was an alpha. A formidable alpha. *Her* alpha.

He relinquished his grasp and walked back into the bedroom. She felt oddly lost, her hand no longer secure in his giant bear-like paw. Shaking if off, she put the plug in and turned on the taps until she had the perfect temperature of water flowing into the giant tub.

"What's this, kitten?" Cord's voice floated over the running water.

"What's what?" Stevie asked turning off the tap before she stepped into her room. When she realised what Cord was holding, she blanched, seeing her face in the mirror behind him, leached of all colour. "N...n...nothing."

His eyes flashed. In his hand, her wand looked so small. He lifted it to his nose, eyes closed, nostrils flared. His lips quirked on one side. "Doesn't smell like nothing to me, kitten." His chest rose with his next inhaled breath. "Smells deliciously like you."

When his tongue darted out to lick it, Stevie bounded across the room, jumping to snatch it out of his hand. "Give it back," she demanded.

His laughter reverberated through the hardwood floors and up into her core, inflaming her clit.

"Why? I thought you said it was nothing." He lifted his hand higher, the toy hovering close to his mouth. "It tastes almost as good as it smells, but certainly not as good as you... hey..."

Stevie had leapt onto the edge of her bed, using it to spring onto his back. Her legs locked around his waist as one hand clutched his neck, while the other scrabbled for the toy.

"Why, you cheeky little minx," he roared with laughter, his free hand fastening around one of her ankles. "Someone needs to teach you a lesson in manners."

Stevie's claws extended, scratching Cord's collar bone.

He hissed between his teeth and, letting go of the toy, seized her hand, extricating her nails from his skin. "Now, now, kitten. Come here."

Cord twisted around and pulled Stevie off his back, tossing her on the bed.

Stevie bounced once, then twice on the mattress; her mouth fell open in a silent gasp. Her core tensed in fervent anticipation.

Cord's lips twitched, and his brow creased. "You need to be taught a lesson, kitten, and it starts now." He bent to cover her mouth with his own in a surprise kiss.

Stevie's eyes fluttered closed, her cat purring so loudly, she drowned out the blood pounding in her ears. She surrendered; her body relaxing into the sheets as Cord's hand traced along her arm.

He plucked the toy out of her limp fingers.

"No satisfaction until you've learned your lesson," he whispered in her ear.

As fast as he had kissed her, he was gone.

Stevie opened her eyes and raised herself onto her elbows, searching for Cord.

She heard the gentle click of the front door latch, confirming he had left, and taken her damn vibrator with him.

CHAPTER THIRTEEN

CORD BUFFETT — OREGON

He'd tossed and turned through what was left of the night, hardly getting a wink of sleep, until with dawn, he finally gave up trying to sleep. Water pelted the taut muscles in his back. Heat seared into his flesh and melted the tension. Internally, his bear thrashed, outraged Cord had walked away from Stevie. Especially when she was so open to being taken by him. In truth, Cord himself wasn't sure why he had left her.

Groaning, he rested his left arm against the tiles of the shower, pillowing his head. He held his half-hard cock in his other hand. From the moment he had met Stevie, she intrigued and irritated him. Her discourteous attitude infuriated him, but it also lent her a level of independence, Cord couldn't help but admire. She certainly hadn't shied away from jumping into danger to save a fellow workmate.

Cord wanted her. His nearly permanent hard-on was testimony enough to that. Initially, the challenge of stealing her away from the pathetic excuse of an alpha heir had been enough for him to overlook Stevie's choice in men, and her sassy nature. She was a brat, and he intended to curb the most offensive elements of her attitude, without detracting from the wild streak which had become both exhilarating and endearing.

Cord refused to listen to the internal ramblings of his bear insisting that Stevie was his mate. He didn't come to Pineville to take a wife. He came to destroy the tribe and exact his revenge for the decades of pain and suffering his mother had suffered because of the selfish machinations of Magda.

His lip curled; a low growl throbbed in his throat. He didn't want to waste a moment more of his thoughts to that witch. He closed his eyes, summoning up the image of Stevie. Her kaftan encasing her petite frame, highlighting her feminine curves and pebbled nipples. Her scent, curling around him, drawing him in.

In his hand, his cock twitched. It grew heavy, and rigid as he thought about Stevie. The softness of her body when she clung to his back, trying to snatch back her vibrator. The fire in her eyes when she was challenged. Her lustrous dark hair, her intrepid spirit. She already knew. Her cat had submitted to his bear long before Cord even began to comprehend there was a true mate in the world for a man like him, let alone that she was standing smack dab in front of him — the antithesis of every other woman he had ever considered attractive.

None held a candle to Stevie's delicate beauty. Even in her hard hat and flannel shirt she stirred his bear.

With a roar, Cord's bear slammed against the front of Cord's mind. The hair on his arms thickened with the pressure of an unwanted change.

The infernal creature within him burned with the need to claim Stevie. Jaw clenched, Cord clamped a hand around his dick. He would fuck Stevie. Not claim her. It had been his intention from the moment he first recognised she was Rygard's woman. Squeezing his dick tighter he pumped the shaft. Stevie was more than just a way to hurt Rygard; to extract revenge.

She was the first woman to stir his lust and captivate his inner beast. A horny monster determined to race off half-cocked to claim a woman they hardly knew.

Cord drew in a ragged breath; attempting to subdue his bear with several strong strokes of his hand. His toes curled, slipping in the water gathered at the bottom of the shower. Just seeing Stevie's face within his mind conjured up the sweetness of her scent. His blood pounded, under his hand, in his ears.

She was theirs.

His bear wouldn't accept anything less from Cord. A quick tumble wouldn't scratch the itch she created.

Groaning, Cord accepted the fact that one night would never be enough to get over the rich allure of Stevie. His bear finally receded, settling back into the depths of Cord's mind with the promise they *would* sink both fang and cock into Stevie's lush body. It didn't take much more pumping of his straining dick to coax the thick spurt of cum to splatter against the shower wall.

Exhaling, Cord relaxed his jaw. His bear finally quiet in his mind. Pushing away from the wall, he allowed the water to sluice over his head, before gathering in his cupped hands. Tossing the water at the wall, he diluted the sticky mess he'd made, allowing it to slide down the tiles and dissipate down the drain with the water. He turned off the tap and stepped out onto the tired old bathmat. He rubbed his face and chest before he slung the towel around his hips and padded out of the pokey bathroom into the main room of his cabin.

Muldoon had insisted that Cord stay in one of his cabins in Pineville. The nearest hotel was a couple of hours drive away and, for the few tourists who ventured close to shifter territory, the dozen or so cabins provided decent accommodation for shifter and human alike.

With the critical eye of a man who made his living in real estate, Cord assessed the worn bones of his temporary home. While clean and serviceable, it wouldn't hurt to be refurbished. His chest pinched; he could picture his mother in this very room, seeing the same faded prints of forested hillsides and fishing bears adorning the walls.

He cringed at the idea of his mother and Ryan together. Logically it had to happen for him to exist but, by all that was holy, he hoped it hadn't been on this bed.

A rapid knock on the door penetrated his musings. Frowning, Cord stood, securing the towel before he cracked open the door.

Muldoon met his scowl with one of his own. "Get dressed. The elders and tribe have called a meeting. Your presence is requested."

Cord raised a brow, his bear bristled at the demand.

The old shifter gulped and cleared his throat. "That is, if you wouldn't mind, Alpha, please will you join the Torben tribe in my bar in ten minutes?"

Cord shut the door in Muldoon's face.

Alpha.

He hated the title. Hated everything it represented. After the encounter with Ryan in the forest, it held a whole new slew of meanings, Cord wasn't ready to face. He didn't want even to face the tribe. His intention was to buy out as many of the tribe as possible, then skip town.

He didn't want to be here to witness the fallout.

When the tribe burned.

And they would burn. He was sure of it.

Shifters were notorious for their territorial nature. They held what they owned with the savageness of their animal instincts. Hating humans almost as much as Cord hated Magda Smith. Yesterday's ambush by the exiled bears attested to that.

Cord knew other tribes or packs were likely to hear about a human corporation buying out shifter assets. He just hadn't expected retaliation by external forces to hit Pineville so swiftly, nor for Stevie to get caught up in their retribution.

Stevie. He had *not* expected her.

Would she attend the meeting? Almost certainly. This spurred him into action. He chose his best suit, shirt and tie from the collection hanging in the wardrobe. Facing the tribe, would be like waging war in the boardroom, something at which he excelled. He was nNotorious in the California business world for being ruthless.

Let the Torben tribe experience this aspect of Cord Buffett's nature. He'd see them all atone for his mother's pain.

He dressed quickly, assessing his appearance in the mirror with a critical eye. He swiped an errant lock of hair off his forehead then reached for his cigar case, lighter and cell. Satisfied, he left the cabin and strode the short distance to Muldoon's Bar. A few young shifters milled around outside, watching the boisterous game the younger kids were playing.

Cord allowed himself a small smile at the sight, tipped his head towards the hushed teens who stared as he past. Halting at the entrance to the bar, he removed a cigar, then slipped the case into his jacket pocket. Lighting the *Puro,* he schooled his features, and opened the door.

The cacophony of voices stopped abruptly when he walked through the crowd. The atmosphere was thick enough to carve, chafing at Cord's bear. With a puff of cigar smoke, his brow drawing tighter, Cord wrapped himself in the familiar sense of power he drew upon in the boardroom.

"This is a no-smoking establishment." A woman reprimanded from the bar.

His gaze sliced to Muldoon, whose mate, Matilda, stood beside him. She clutched a rag in one hand, Scotch glass in the other and, despite her firm voice, Cord detected an aura of nervousness. Taking a long drag, Cord pinched the cigar between his thumb and forefinger, removed it from his mouth and, slowly, blew a ring of smoke. It formed a solid white doughnut in front of his face, then caught the lazy current of air and floated towards the older woman. The outline ruffled as it expanded in size, and decreased in colour, evaporating just in front of the bar.

Matilda didn't disguise her animosity, yet with Muldoon's hand over her wrist, she refrained from hurling what was undoubtably an acerbic retort.

A small part of him respected the woman — his mother's great aunt — albeit grudgingly, at her refusal to be cowed by him. It was swamped by the deep-seated antipathy, which had increased in direct proportion to his mother's anguished withdrawal as he grew into his bear. While she had not hated shifters, they terrified her. Haunted by her encounter. Here. In this town. In this bar. With these people.

He hardened his heart. They deserved to pay for his mother's torment. The whole damned lot of them. Maybe then she could rest in peace.

His bear countered, *How do you know she* isn't *at peace?*
The only person who deserves to be destroyed is Magda. The tribe
didn't know, no one knew.

The front door swung open. The hair on his nape prickled
with the groundswell of power accompanying the flurry
of fresh air. Cord didn't need to turn to recognise the
arrival of Ryan or hear the ensuing gasps and whispered
exclamations.

"Alpha."

"Settle down, people." Magda's sickly-sweet voice
intruded. "Settle down. Come on, settle down, now."

Cord strove to keep his expression blank. His bear wanted
to tear out Magda's throat. He made do with glaring daggers
at the woman he hated most in the world.

Magda wore red. From the figure-hugging dress, and
matching bag over her shoulder, to the peep-toe, heeled
shoes, and painted lips. She oozed confidence, exploiting
what she considered to be sex appeal, and her position as
the alpha's mate. A woman, secure in her own body and her
position in life.

Ryan filled the void of the sunlit doorway. His broad
frame now clothed in jeans and a worn leather jacket over
a black T-shirt. Unbridled authority flowed from his bear,
permeating the room, and enveloping the tribe. Yet his eyes
were glazed.

Whatever had transpired after Cord and Stevie left Ryan
and his son in the forest, Magda had been able to reinforce

her claim. Cord had seen enough vacant-minded people in California to recognise a drug-induced mental state when he saw one.

The door closed as Rygard slunk around Ryan, melting into the crowd. He might know how to fight, but he lacked the command of an alpha.

I am alpha. His bear was calm in his mind. For once, they were in unison. Rygard posed no threat to them. Only Magda. Ryan's bear had already submitted to Cord, and why he was here now, as human as the day he was born, his bear trapped once more under whatever spell Magda had woven over him.

Offended by Magda's cloying scent, Cord sucked smoke deep into his lungs, and exhaled in the witch's direction.

Her nose wrinkled, and her mouth pinched when the grey haze coiled around her head. She waved at the smoke with one hand. "Cord, this is a no-smoking establishment. Put that filthy thing out."

"Make me." Cord repeated the gesture.

"Ryan," Magda whined like a spoiled child. "Make him stub out that disgusting cigar."

Ryan stepped towards Cord, there was a momentary glint in his glassy eyes. The bear was trying to fight through Magda's power over him.

Cord straightened his spine and squared his shoulders. Tilting up his head, he blew another plume of smoke, this time into Ryan's face.

The older male blinked and closed his eyes, his nostrils quivering at the pungent vapour gliding across his skin. His head jerked and when he opened his eyes, the essence of Ryan's inner bear was stronger. "Leave the man be. If he wants to smoke, let him."

Magda gawped at her mate.

Cord glowered at her; certain Ryan had denied her nothing since the day she stole him from Lizzie.

He dismissed her, and asked Muldoon, "Okay, you asked me to come. Here I am. Get on with it. I have far more pressing matters to attend to than slumming it with this crowd."

Magda snatched his arm. "How dare you make any demands on this tribe and its council of elders."

Cord's head whipped around, and he bared his teeth. "Remove your hand."

"Leave him be, Magda." Ryan lifted his mate's hand off Cord, then looked around the room. "The Torben tribe has suffered a great loss over the years, which has weakened us, nearly destroyed us. It still might."

A murmur rippled around the room. Cord frowned, wondering where Ryan was going with this.

A chair scraped the wooden floor followed by a screech, "It all started with that witch."

Magda gasped. "How dare yo—"

Ryan clamped a hand over her mouth. "Quiet, woman."

Cord's gaze landed on the exiled bear whom he had fought to save Stevie. His bear wanted to explode out of him, to finish off the bastard who dared return to tribal lands, come near Stevie again.

Ryan shouldered past Cord to stab his finger in the direction of the interloper. "You've already been banished by me and were banished again last night by the alpha."

Heat chased down Cord's spine.

The crowd erupted.

"What?" hissed Magda, barely heard over the ruckus.

"Quiet," roared Ryan. His power pulsed around the bar, subduing the tribe.

"Nearly thirty years ago, I met my true mate, but I was blind, and didn't recognise how special she was. She left Pineville before I woke up to myself and, instead of chasing after her and taking her for my mate, I claimed Magda. Despite that, I shared a bond with my true mate, so strong that when she died, my bear snapped, and I lost control of him." Ryan rubbed the back of his neck and looked at Cord. "Only when I came face to face with that bond was I able to regain control. My bear submitted, surrendering his position as alpha to Cord. My true heir. A son born of my true mate."

Stunned exclamations, shocked gasps, and astonished whispers blended into a single, unintelligible noise.

"No!"

Cord heard Stevie clear over the din. He searched for her, but all he could see was a press of bear-shifters. Ice skewered his side, the numbness exploding into pain. He stared in disbelief at the decorative knife handle protruding from his body.

CHAPTER FOURTEEN

STEVIE RAHAL — OREGON

The tension amongst the tribe, filling Muldoon's Bar, was palpable. Stevie had never seen so many shifters jammed into one space before. It made getting close to Cord difficult, especially since she had arrived late. At least Timmo had thought to send her a message, otherwise she wouldn't be here at all.

Stevie hated being short when she had to navigate crowds, made worse when giant bear shifters towered over her. No one paid her any notice, as she shoved through the throng.

Ryan's announcement echoed in the sudden hush. His tribe hung off every word. "My true heir. A son born of my true mate."

The crowd surged forward. Stevie, her ears ringing, stumbled, putting her hand out to prevent an ignominious face plant.

She looked up, her gaze level with Magda's handbag, spotting the older woman withdrawing her hand from its depths. Light glinted off the sharp edge of a wavy-shaped blade. Magda's knuckles whitened as her fingers gripped the decorative handle of the knife.

Magda's features were contorted with rage, and the alpha's mate was fixated on Cord. Dread flooded Stevie's system; her cat's hackles stood on end.

"No," Stevie yelled. She lurched upwards to snag Magda around her waist, tackling her to the floor.

Hands slapped at her head, fingers drilled into her hair, ripping at the roots.

Stevie hissed and her claws, unsheathed with her partial shift, gouged into Magda's hips.

Hauled off her quarry, hair rent from her scalp, Stevie's talons sliced through flesh and tore open Magda's dress. Flailing for purchase, Stevie found her back braced against a hard chest, a pair of strong arms circling her middle. She scrabbled to resume treating Magda as her very own scratching post.

"Enough, kitten."

Electricity zipped through her at the almost imperceptible caress against the shell of her ear. Panting, Stevie stopped thrashing. Cigar and sandalwood filled her nose.

"Cord?" His name fell from her lips in a breathless whisper. She wiggled, attempting to turn in his arms. "She was going to stab you, I had to stop her—"

Cord's eyes closed, and he grimaced. "Yeah, stop jiggling about, kitten. You're killin' me here." He dropped one hand to his right side, while the other held her tight to his body.

The metallic odour of blood cut through the cigar smoke. "I wasn't fast enough? Let me down, Cord. Let me see what damage that bitch has caused." She pushed against his shoulder, writhing to see the wound.

He slid Stevie down his body, only releasing her when her feet hit the floor.

Stevie's hand hovered over the handle protruding from Cord's side. "If she was aiming for your kidney, she missed. I'm just not sure whether she nicked your liver." Gingerly, Stevie grasped the leather-bound handle. "I saw the blade, it's got a wicked set of curves on it, all wavy like. I can pull it out if you want, but it'll hurt, and if your liver is damaged, you'll need to shift to accelerate your healing. I don't need you bleeding out on me."

Cord swayed.

Ryan appeared beside him, clapping a big-beefy hand on Cord's shoulder, bolstering him.

"Where's Magda?" he boomed.

Stevie looked to where she had been dragged away from Magda. The woman was nowhere to be seen.

The tribe shared nervous glances, but no one answered.

"Find her, bring her back. She made an unprovoked attack on my son, she must face tribal law," Ryan growled.

When no one moved fast enough, the old alpha roared, "*Now*."

In a ruckus of chairs scraping and tabled banging, the room emptied, leaving Ryan and Stevie with Cord. Rygard loitered near the door, while Muldoon and Matilda bustled behind the bar.

Ryan spotted Rygard. With a jerk of his head, he beckoned his younger son. "Did you see your mother leave?"

Rygard shook his head.

"Will you help find her?"

Another shake.

Ryan's deep breath through his nose was loud enough to share his displeasure. "You can help here then. Move the tables and chairs out of the way, Cord needs space to shift."

Grinding his teeth, Rygard hesitated, then caught sight of Stevie's red-rimmed eyes. Rolling his head, he cracked his neck and set to relocating the bar's furnishings.

Muldoon approached, a freshly opened bottle of Jack Daniel's in one hand, a clean towel in the other. "Here, boy, drink this. It'll help numb the pain."

Cord took the bottle and downed half the contents in several large gulps.

Stevie hadn't taken her eyes off Cord. She monitored his wan complexion. Watched the bob of his Adam's apple when he guzzled the whiskey. When he lowered the bottle, Stevie yanked out the knife.

Muldoon pressed the towel on the wound, the second the bloodied blade was clear.

Cord collapsed onto his knees with an agonised bellow.

"Shift," ordered Ryan.

The air sizzled, churning with the conflicting power of the two alphas. Cord's bear, in his weakened state, submitted. Convulsing, man became beast, shredding Cord's clothes in the process, the shift more awkward with the injury.

His bright, shining eyes opened and closed slowly. The huge Kodiak kept his gaze on Stevie, who choked back a sob, her lips trembling with the effort to smile. Burrowing her fingers into his thick fur, she steadied herself.

The towel in Muldoon's hand was almost black with the iron-rich blood seeping from the lacerated liver. It was now a waiting game.

Could Cord's shifter nature reverse the damage before he bled out?

⁂

A persistent rap on the door woke Stevie. She blinked away her disorientation and groaned at the stiffness in her neck. Cord was stretched out on the bed, a sheet pulled up to his waist, chest bare. The harsh lines of his face were softened in slumber. His colour had returned to Stevie's relief.

The tapping resumed. Briefly, Cord's forehead creased into a frown.

"Hang on a blasted minute will ya," Stevie mumbled. Rising from the chair she had carried to the side of the bed, she padded to the door, and cracked it open to see Rygard's fist about to bang the wood again.

His eyes bulged and he stepped back. "Dad sent me."

Stevie glanced at Cord, confirming he hadn't stirred. She crept outside and pulled the door to. "Go on."

"They found Mom. The tribe is being recalled. There will be another attempt to conduct the tribal meeting in an hour. D'you reckon," he jutted his chin towards the cabin, "he'll wake by then or what?"

Refusing to look at Rygard, Stevie gave a half shrug. "His pallor has improved. He's sleeping peacefully at the moment, and he's strong," she peeked at him from under her lashes, "Powerful. He'll recover, I'm sure. We'll join the meeting as soon as he feels up to it."

She was about to go back inside, when Rygard reached for her hand, thwarting her retreat. "Wait."

Stevie jerked her arm free. "What?" she demanded.

He rubbed his eye before raking his fingers through his hair, scratching his scalp. "I...look...it was wrong of me to bite you. I...I'm sorry, okay?"

"It's not okay." She spun on her heel to punch him in the arm. "You don't get to sink your blasted teeth into me, faking a claim, in front of my *mate*, and think all you have to do is apologise and everything will be back to normal."

She eased the door open a couple of inches, and turned, her gaze boring into Rygard. "You should know, I want to kill your mother for stabbing Cord. Tribal law or not, if the council of elders don't see fit to hand her a death sentence, I will kill her myself, and it won't be pretty. Cats like to toy with their prey."

She saw his face drain of all colour, then walked into the cabin and, with the softest of clicks, shut the door on him. Leaning against the wood panelling, eyes closed, Stevie drew a deep breath, in through her nose, and out through her mouth, repeating the pattern until her inner cat settled, and her heart stopped hammering.

She exhaled on a loud sigh.

"You can't kill Magda."

Stevie's eyes snapped open, and she crossed to the bed. "Cord," she purred his name. "You're awake."

He was propped up on one elbow, his brooding expression relaxing into the merest hint of a smile. "I am."

An undeniable force bound them. He was magnetic, and no matter how hard she tried, she couldn't keep any distance between them. She tucked a loose strand of hair behind her ear and perched on the bottom of his bed. "Why can't I kill Magda?" she asked. His clean, masculine scent enveloped her. The spicy aroma of sandalwood balanced by the smoky, almost sweet notes of his cigars.

He crooked a finger at her, beckoning her closer.

She arched an eyebrow and shook her head. "Tell me why not, Cord."

His face darkened; eyes almost hidden beneath his frown. "Because she's mine to kill."

Stevie reached under the bed sheet, running her hand over his toes until she cupped the ball of his foot. Her fingers worked over the thick ridges of the bones in his foot, her thumb dug in below his big toe. She held Cord's gaze. "Why?"

He wiggled his toes under her ministrations, but slumped back on to the bed, throwing an arm over his face. "I don't want to talk about it."

She seized his little toe and waggled it between her thumb and forefinger.

He growled at her. "Watch it, kitten."

She rolled her eyes and pinched his toe. "Tell me."

"Do that again, and I *will* spank you," he promised.

Stevie squirmed with the image *that* vow spawned. "Don't change the subject," she croaked.

He moved his arm and lifted his head. Eyes gleaming, he stared hard at her. "You like that idea, don't you, kitten?"

She looked at his toe still in her hand. "I'll tell you if you tell me."

Cord snorted. "Brat," he murmured. He huffed a breath, expelling it in a rush. "She lied to my mother. Filling her with so much fear she left. Left her mate, left her family, never went near another shifter again... at least until I turned thirteen and shifted for the first time. I watched her pull away from me, her nightmares manifesting until she could barely look at me anymore. She was happy with my father — the man who raised me — but something was always missing from her life, we just didn't know what, or why."

He stretched out one arm, in obvious invitation, and Stevie crawled across the covers to slip her hand into his.

Gathering her close, Cord pillowed her head on his chest, one hand entwined in her hair while the fingertips of his other hand trailed up and down her arm, absently. "Muldoon's mate, Matilda is...was my mother's great aunt. She was staying here during a university break and met Ryan. He swept her off her feet. Muldoon and Matilda believed they were true mates but, without warning, my mother vanished one night, and the only contact they had from here again was a letter, she had arranged for them to receive sometime after her death, in which she told them I was a bear. That was when Muldoon realised I was the son of Ryan Jones., and he tracked me down in California."

Cord's fingers got caught in a knot, he paused his explanation to work her hair free. Once he could glide his fingers through her tresses again, he continued, "After a heated discussion, I relayed the story of why mother left Pineville. Between us, we established that Magda had set her sights on Ryan, was determined to have him, and be claimed by him. My mother was a rival, the spanner in the works and, to get rid of her, Magda spun so many lies, my mother left

Pineville terrified of shifters. I swore on her grave I would seek vengeance, allowing her to rest in peace."

A chill bloomed across Stevie's skin, and she shuddered. "Is that what brought you to Pineville?"

His hand in her hair, stilled. "Muldoon wanted me to save the tribe." He grunted, "Honestly, as far as I'm concerned, the lot of 'em can burn in hell."

Stevie levered herself up to meet Cord's gaze. "This is my tribe too, Cord. Do you want me to burn with them?"

"No—"

"Do you truly want to hold nearly a hundred innocent people to account for a matter they have zero knowledge of?

Stevie pressed a finger to his lips. "I understand why you want Magda dead, frankly, so do I, but I can't condone the wanton destruction of the tribe, an innocent community who took me in and gave me a home when I was in need of one."

Cord nipped her finger. She yelped, tugging it away from his mouth.

"I changed my mind." He spoke.

"Good," she started to smile, then frowned. "Wait.... what about your mind did you change?"

He cupped her face, a gentle smile played on his face. "Stevie, Stevie. My Stevie," he murmured. "Magda is the one who needs to pay, and while my bear and I love the idea of your cat drawing out her death, I cannot allow you to do that."

"Why not?"

"Because."

Stevie's gaze locked with Cord's, seeing his eyes flash with the light of his inner bear. "Because?" she drew out the question.

"Because, I said so, and I expect to be obeyed," Cord's tone was implacable.

Her mouth went dry, all the moisture her body possessed had pooled in her panties at the dominance he wielded in those few words.

CHAPTER FIFTEEN

CORD BUFFETT — OREGON

Her arousal was the sweetest scent he'd ever inhaled. Cord skimmed a hand across Stevie's jaw, revelling in the silky softness of her skin. He lifted onto his elbow, their faces, inches apart. She was irresistible. Even his bear, drowsing in his mind, was drawn to her.

He needed her.

The luminous beauty of her bright-eyed stare trapped him. The tip of her pink tongue, gliding across her lower lip, seduced him. The soft flutter of her tremulous breath against his mouth, tormented him. The pressure of his fingers behind her ear increased infinitesimally, his thumb tracing the sharp angle of her cheek bone.

She responded, welcoming his tender kiss. Pliant lips yielded under his as she matched his passion, sharing the kiss, rather than surrendering to his control.

He smiled, a bubble of mirth breaking the moment. He peppered her mouth with featherlight kisses, then leaned away with a roguish grin.

"You ever taken dance lessons?" he tossed the question at her, catching her off guard.

Eyebrows arched above puzzled brown eyes. "What?"

He grazed his thumb across her lower lip. "You don't follow the lead, do you?"

Her blush highlighted the faintest smattering of freckles on her cheeks. She took his hand from her face and entwined their fingers. "You should take a shower and get dressed. The tribe will be gathering soon. Magda will be tried before the council of elders. Whatever business necessitated the earlier meeting may or may not take place depending on what happens."

Cord stared at Stevie, the speed at which her thoughts jetted off on a tangent, made his head spin.

She raised their clasped hands and brushed a gentle kiss to his knuckles. "We haven't time for you to teach me how to dance." Stevie released his hand and scrambled off the bed.

About to follow, Cord was hindered by an acute spasm in his back. His body had healed, but the phantom pain of the injury reminded him he was still mortal. He closed his eyes and sucked in a deep breath. When he finally took Stevie, he wanted to be on his game, not stymied by this damned wound and aching body. She deserved nothing less, especially after the way she'd flown at Magda. The loyal little spitfire was a treasure to be worshipped, every which way he could and then some.

Huffing out a breath that ruffled the lock of hair on his forehead, Cord threw back the sheet. He was stiff getting out of bed, but once on his feet, he steadied.

Stevie, peeking through the curtains, heard his gasp, and glanced over, biting her lower lip.

He padded to where she stood and smoothed the maligned flesh with his thumb. He nodded towards the other side of the room. "Why don't you find me some clothes while I shower? Unless of course you want to join me?"

Her laughter floated across the cabin caressing his cock, making the heavy length twitch. "Just go shower will you."

"Fine, but I'll leave the door open in case you change your mind." He walked to the bathroom backwards, granting Stevie full view of his erection when she turned from the window.

Her breath caught in her throat. She reached for a pillow and tossed it at him with a choked giggle. "Cord. You're terrible."

Cord caught the pillow with a snort. Shaking his head, he tossed it on the end of the bed and sauntered into the bathroom. He turned on the mixer tap in the shower, setting the temperature to a comfortable heat. Stevie would follow him in. He was sure of it. He could smell the fresh flood of her arousal permeating the cabin.

His skin tingled. Stevie's small hand cupped him, rolling his leaden balls between her fingers. With a groan, Cord closed his eyes and moved so Stevie could step in front of him.

Stevie's free hand circled his dick. It throbbed in her careful grasp. Her tongue teased the slit of the bulbous head, stretching the opening.

Cord hissed. His fingers danced across the top of Stevie's head, sweeping over the silken strands until he found her ponytail, and tugged her head away before she could take more than the tip of him into her hot mouth.

"Not now, kitten." Cord opened his eyes to look at her. Naked and bowed towards him, her wide eyes were almost luminous in the incandescent light of the bathroom bulb. His aching length bobbed close to her mouth, almost like his body had a will of its own to be taken by the pretty little cat shifter at his feet. "I want to make something very clear. This isn't a bit of fun now, Stevie. If we take this any further, you *will* submit to me. I *will* claim you. You *will* be *mine* and only *mine*. I will dominate, I will fuck, and I will punish if you deserve it."

She never blinked. Her bosom heaved with her ragged breathing.

With a jerk of his head, and the gentle pressure of his hand entangled in her hair, Cord commanded her to stand up.

Stevie obeyed, but her impish nature manifested, and she slid his dick between her breasts as she got to her feet, sandwiching his rigid shaft.

Cord dragged in a shuddering breath, his hand knotted in her hair until he arched her head back, exposing the delicate column of her neck to his hungry gaze. His bear roared in his head, determined to claim her now.

"Are you listening to me, Stevie?"

She swallowed, her throat working with the awkwardness of the angle. She squeezed him harder between her boobs, her fingers kneading her skin. "I am."

His lip trembled with the effort of controlling a snarl. "You *will* obey me, kitten. I will fuck you when *I* want, how *I* want. I *will* own every inch of your body including that sassy mouth of yours not to mention your sweet pussy and ass."

"My Alpha," she moaned her eyes glazing over, lids half closed.

Cord bent closer. "You're going to scream my name as I claim your body, sink my teeth into you and sear your soul with my cum," he promised.

Her eyes rolled back in her head. The aromatic evidence of her arousal grew heavier in the damp air of the now steamy bathroom. "Yes," she husked

He pulled his cock free from her breasts, eliciting a whimper from her as he stepped away into the shower. He drew her with him, manoeuvring her under the cascade of water. His free hand ghosted across the curve of one boob until he had her taut nipple rolling between his thumb and forefinger.

He bent to capture her lips with his own. His kiss was hard, stealing her breath. Their tongues tangled, fighting for dominance.

She was his and he would erase any memory of any other man she had experienced before him.

Cord released her hair, to skim his hand down her spine, imprinting every bump and curve of into his memory. Coming to the firm swell of her buttocks, he massaged the flesh, his palm itching to spank her, to brand her, but he restrained himself. They had a lifetime ahead of them. She would require disciplining frequently...of that he had no doubt. Her ass would glow with the print of his hand soon enough.

Cord moved lower until his fingers pressed into the solid muscle of her thigh. She wasn't just toned to his touch. Her body was athletic, muscled with the strength of not only a shifter, but a woman who did not shy away from manual labour. A heavier press of his fingertips had her responding to his unspoken command, her leg hitched up his leg.

His hard cock rested against her belly; the sensitive tip rubbed along the underneath of her boob. A growl rumbled in the back of his throat.

He released her nipple, gliding his hand down her ribs to her hip. With the other hand under her knee, he hoisted her up.

She gasped against his lips. Claws dug into his flesh, her legs hooked around his hips, her pussy slid across the head of his dick.

Cord groaned. His fingers flexing against her body. He released her mouth.

"Last chance, kitten. Once I'm inside you, you'll be mine forever," his voice was hoarse, gruffer than he expected.

Stevie slid one hand between them, and squeezed him once, twice. "Take me, Alpha. I'm yours forever."

His bear pushed forward, desperate to sever Cord's mental reins, but Cord maintained control and thrust his dick past the slick folds of her pussy and into her pulsing, hot, wet core.

Her head dropped back, one hand clawing at the hard planes of the back of his shoulder. The other hand tracing the hard ridges of his abdomen until she palmed one of his pecs.

Cord pushed her against the wall and peeled her hand from his chest. There would come a time when he would let her trace his body, use him however she desired but, right now, he was struggling to hold back his bear. He needed to lead this dance. He couldn't afford the luxury of letting Stevie undermine his control.

He interlaced their fingers, his hand dwarfing hers, and pinned it to the wall, level with her shoulder.

Cord flexed his hips, cold air rushed around every inch of his length as he pulled out of Stevie's body. The taut muscles of her pussy clamped around the head of his dick, refusing to let him go. Shuffling his feet through the warm water pooling around his ankles, Cord thrust back in until he had Stevie's clit grinding against his pubic arch.

His control was slipping.

Her pussy convulsing around his dick was exquisite torture. Cord withdrew once more, finding the pace which allowed him to pound into Stevie's body to gain the maximum effect.

The exquisite pain of her sharp claws, clinging to his shoulder, enhanced his pleasure. His belly clenched, and his balls drew preparing for his release.

Cord had never experienced anything like it. The need to cum rocketed through him, but he couldn't.

Not yet.

He wanted — no — needed Stevie to be right up there with him. This was a journey they had to take together.

He alternated between deep, firm thrusts, to shallow, slow thrusts. He used every inch of his cock to torment her body, searching for the g-spot, that magic place that would send her spiralling over the edge.

When the head of his cock nudged over a knot in her spasming walls, she gasped in his ear. Cord repeated the motion.

Stevie moaned.

Cord moved a little faster, pressed a little harder.

Her moan became more of a keen, her breathing grew ragged, and her bosom shuddered against his chest. His rhythm intensified.

"C...C...C...Cor...Cor...Cor..."

His bear merged with him. As one, the two moved in concert.

Stevie was theirs.

Their mate.

The other half of their shared soul.

His canines extended. With a roar, he sank his fangs into the delicate skin where Stevie's neck met her shoulder. He drank the sweet taste of her blood, greedy with every gulp he took.

"Cord," she screamed his name. Her pussy strangled his dick, contracting so hard he almost couldn't move.

He thrust again.

Once.

Twice.

His orgasm ripped through him. Thick, hot spurts of cum pumped out of his throbbing dick. His teeth receded, releasing her tender skin.

Stevie's pussy pulsed around his highly sensitive flesh, their mingled juices dribbled down his cock, sliding over his balls to mingle with the hot water of the shower. Her body trembled in his arms. Her head fell forward and bumped his shoulder.

His legs shook and his mind spun. There was something else subsuming him. The soft magic of a mating bond, cushioning him, suffusing his body, branding his soul, owning him.

Stevie was his.

He was hers.

"You're mine now, Stevie. Mine to hold, mine to cherish, mine to love."

She squeezed his hand.

Once.

Twice.

Three times.

"I'm also yours, Stevie. Come what may, I'm yours."

Glassy eyes refocused on his face, and her lips curved into a sweet smile.

Cord felt a sense of completeness, something he hadn't known he was missing until this moment.

CHAPTER SIXTEEN

CORD AND STEVIE — OREGON

Stevie watched Cord dress. She fidgeted where she sat in the chair, back in its spot in the corner of the room. She couldn't believe she found it erotic. The way he pulled his slacks on. Snapping his shirt open; the little flair to the way he flung it around him, the crisp white cotton sliding over his tanned skin. Every button was caressed by those heavy-set fingers that had tweaked and teased her nipples, as, nimbly, he threaded them into the corresponding buttonhole.

He looped his tie around his neck.

Stevie bit her lip, her skin tingled with the fantasy of that same silk tie being drawn around her flesh. Securing her. Bending her to Cord's will. He could, and would, have his own way with her. The idea of her complete submission scared and exhilarated her. Within her, her cat purred, curled up within her mental walls like a damn domesticated pet.

Cord was her match in every way, taking control of the situation, her body, her mind. His all-consuming power had allowed her to lose herself in the moment, surrendering to the crescendo of her arousal, sinking into the depths of their shared passion. He kept her anchored whilst pushing her beyond her boundaries until her soul shattered around her. The force of her orgasm had left her boneless. If it hadn't been for the strong arms cradling her, the whispered words of affirmation, she may have been lost to the spiritual realm.

"Where's my watch?"

Cord's voice cracked the haze of Stevie's fantasy.

"Huh?" She blinked.

He gave her a crooked grin and straightened the sleeves of his shirt under his jacket. He tapped his wrist. "My watch. Where is it?"

"Oh." Stevie frowned, *when had he donned his jacket?* "The strap broke when you shifted in the bar to heal. I think Mattie collected the pieces. There is a jeweller in the tribe, I think she was going to see whether she could get it repaired for you."

He nodded briskly, as he removed a small leather carry-on bag from the wardrobe. He unzipped it around and lifted the lid.

Stevie couldn't drag her gaze away from the way his hands flexed while he rifled through the contents. He retrieved a fancy looking box with a clear cover. With the same efficient movements, he had used to get dressed, he opened the box and withdrew something shiny.

Cord slipped a gold watch over his wrist. "I always carry a spare," he explained. He glanced at the time on the face, then across at the ugly red digital display on the clock radio beside the bed. "The winder keeps the movement running."

Stevie's eyebrows rose. "The winder?"

He twisted his hand around, showing her the box briefly before he replaced it in his bag. "That's just the travel size one. I have a larger collection at home, in a much bigger winder box."

She half-shrugged. "I just use my phone to tell the time. A watch would just get in the way on site. Hell." She held up her bare hands turning them about to show him the backs as well as her palms. "I don't wear jewellery of any description."

Cord stalked towards her, captured her hand and moulded her flush to his hard body. She felt his large fingers settle around her throat, his thumb stroking the pulse point in her neck, throbbing wildly at his touch. "I'd love to see you dripping in pearls."

Visualising the kind of 'pearls' he would massage in after splattering them against her skin, heat coiled outwards from her centre.

His hand tightened a fraction around her neck, brows furrowed over his dark eyes. "Careful, kitten. Keep your mind out of the gutter, or I'll have to punish you."

"What? I didn't say anything," she protested breathlessly.

He dropped a kiss on her forehead. "You didn't have to. Not only are your naughty thoughts written all over your face," he quipped, "they're stronger than any perfume."

She gasped and was about to object when a knock halted her.

Cord released her to answer the door.

Stevie felt bereft without the heat of his fingers against her skin, the intimacy of their moment broken by the deep murmur of a male voice outside.

"Kitten?" Cord stretched out a hand.

The tribe were waiting for them. The memory of Magda sinking her stupid knife into Cord's back was a bucket of ice-cold water over her libido. Stevie rolled her head from side to side, loosening the knots. Two steps and her hand was engulfed in Cord's. He ushered her outside where she came face-to-face with Timmo. The old lumberjack's eyes widened in shock when he spotted the distinctive mating scar on her neck.

"No wonder Rygard sent me when the alpha asked him to come check whether Cord was awake." He glanced at Cord, "You didn't waste any time staking your claim. Well, come on. The tribe has assembled, and Magda is ready to spit fire in there."

Cord's hand squeezed hers.

Stevie reciprocated — three times, recalling her dad doing the same when she was a child, telling her three presses of her hand was a silent way of saying 'I love you'.

Cord closed and locked the door, and the trio descended the steps for the short walk to Muldoon's Bar.

The humidity was oppressive, exacerbating an atmosphere already strained, and enveloping Stevie with the uncomfortable disquiet normally associated with funerals.

Timmo pushed the door and entered the bar holding it back for Cord and Stevie to follow. The drone of the overhead fans was louder than the buzz of conversation, as the aging machines tried to stir the sultry air with minimal success, and certainly did nothing to alleviate the tension Stevie felt when all eyes swivelled in her direction.

Wordlessly, those tribal members on their feet, parted, making room for the three to walk to the platform at the far side of the bar where the council of elders was already seated, Ryan standing alongside.

Gagged and tied to a chair in front of the council, Magda glared daggers at them. There was no love lost there. At a table near the dais, among the men she worked with and their families, Rygard scowled, his eyes averted, his affectionate demeanour, long gone.

The BearHeart Logging crew shared confused glances until Timmo resumed his seat. Stevie noticed him mutter something in the ear of the man next to him. Like a child's game of Chinese Whispers blended with a Mexican wave, their expressions morphed from bewildered to surprised, as the information, which, she suspected related to her being mated to Cord was passed among the tribe.

"I trust you have recovered, Cord?"

Ryan's question reached every nook and cranny of the bar. His innate authority as alpha brought Stevie's attention back to the reason they were here. Magda was on trial for attempted murder.

"Yeah. I'm good as new." Cord glowered at Magda. "Despite your best efforts to the contrary."

Ryan nodded. "Good." He cleared his throat. "Then this council will convene before the entire tribe to resolve two matters of utmost importance."

Cord lifted his hand, still holding Stevie's, to check his watch. "I hope this won't take long. I have a plane to catch."

"What?" Stevie hissed, making a futile attempt to extricate her fingers. Cord simply refused to let go.

Magda tossed her head, muffled noises emanated from behind her gag.

Ryan stepped towards him. "What plane? Why? You only just arrived in town. Your challenge—"

Cord interrupted, scoffing, "I didn't come here to challenge *you*, alpha. I came to see *her*—" his features hardened when looked at Magda, "—pay for what she did to my mother. The greedy bitch did all the work for me."

Cord scanned the crowd of unfamiliar faces. Not just the men, whole families, they were all here, hanging off his every word. Words which had the power to destroy or to save. This wasn't the boardroom of a business he wanted to take over. Stevie's luminous eyes, large in her beautiful face, stared up at him, brimming with un-shed tears, and her hand trembled in his.

"I had no intention of coming here. Not at first anyway." Cord addressed Stevie, although everyone heard his words. "When Muldoon visited me in California, when he told me Ryan had gone mad after my mother's death, and that Magda was destroying the tribe, I didn't care. The tribe could burn in Hell for all I cared. At first."

A murmur rippled out from those gathered, a couple of gasps, the odd curse or two.

He ignored them, his focus on Stevie. "In the end, I couldn't help myself. I set my assistant the task of researching Pineville and the assets of the Torben tribe. Muldoon was right. The tribe was a mess. The contracts transferring ownership to the tribal council were labyrinthine.

"While the Better Business Bureau had the Torben tribe listed as owners of over ninety percent of the tribe's assets, a little digging revealed that Magda held the title for the majority of current and past businesses owned by the tribe, which were haemorrhaging money.

"It didn't take much for me to persuade my brother to devise a takeover package. To extend the range of BPG outside California."

Magda renewed her efforts to dislodge the gag, desperate to be heard against the rising tide of outrage.

"Had Benny not been on his honeymoon, he would be the one finalising the takeover. The slut was holding out for a face-to-face. Plus—" Cord chided, his gaze swinging to a sulking Rygard, "—no one could get hold of BearHeart Logging to discuss buying them out. So here I am.

"It was easier to get Magda to sign the contracts than it was to keep her slimy hands off me. I admit, I was surprised at how fast the news of the buyout, once I had what I came for—"

He was cut off by the exclamations of wrath exploding from the throng. Stevie shrank from the noise, unable to understand a single word the raucous voices were yelling one over another.

"Quiet," Ryan's voice cut through the din, his alpha power cracked like lightening across the crowd. "What *did* you come for?"

Cord regarded his sire. "Initially? I wanted this tribe obliterated—"

Ryan raised his hands, commanding silence before the tribe could react.

"You were right," Cord looked back at Stevie, "the tribe isn't at fault for the actions of one woman. I must return to Glendale, to set things right. I can't dissolve the contracts. Buffett Property Group are the legal owners of the tribal assets. Restitution of property and/or businesses to the rightful owners, should they wish to regain possession, will require, at the very least, deeds of covenant. It's not a quick fix, it'll take time, and I can't tackle it remotely, the board... just trust me on this, okay, kitten?"

"Cord?" Ryan caught his attention. "Will you please confirm your intentions for this tribe ... your tribe? I submitted to your challenge, as far as I am concerned, you are the rightful alpha of the Torben shifters."

"The Torben tribe will be restored to its former strength. Any loyal shifter families, deprived of their livelihood or who were forced into exile owing to Magda's machinations will, eventually, have what was taken, restored."

"How?" An angry voice demanded from the opposite side of the bar.

Cord bit back a growl when he recognised the exiled bear shifter.

The other bear shouldered his way through the crowd until he stood four feet from Cord. "How can any of the families who were screwed over by that witch claim *anything*? You said yourself you can't rip up the contracts, so what? Your *human* company will cop a loss to just return ownership to shifters? I don't think so. We can't afford to buy them back," he sneered. "You talk big, Mr Slick, in your fancy suit, but you stink of bullshit."

Cord' smirked. "I intend to honour the bills of sale. The money will go directly to the tribe, as per the terms of the contracts. I shall work with the council of elders to establish a committee who will assess every application for the money required to redeem their titles."

Magda sounded as though she was laughing hysterically, even muffled by the gag.

Cord peeled his hand away from Stevie's. He walked over to Magda, bending over until he was almost nose to nose with her. "Sorry, bitch, you should have read the fine print. You were transferring *your* ownership to Buffett Property Group. The financial remuneration was to be paid into a trust fund only accessible by the Torben council of elders, bypassing you entirely. You were never going to see a damn cent."

She fought against her bonds and, somehow working her gag free, shrieked, "You bastard. I should have killed your whore of a mother rather than just chase her of—"

Magda's poisonous vitriol was reduced to a ghastly gurgle.

A hot, sticky substance sprayed Cord's face. His lip twisted into a vicious snarl, and his incensed gaze met Ryan's.

The older shifter stood beside his dead mate. Deadly, thick, black bear claws curved from distended, hairy fingers, dripping with blood.

Cord was furious. "You killed her."

Ryan retorted brusquely, "We all witnessed her attack on the alpha of this tribe. It was a foregone conclusion she would be found guilty by the council of elders. As her mate, it was my responsibility to administer justice."

Wiping the blood from his face, Cord flicked it off his fingers onto Magda, hanging limp and dishevelled within the ropes surrounding her body. He spat the vile taste of her blood from his mouth before he walked away.

He stopped next to Stevie and, for her ears only, exhorted, "Come back to California with me?"

Without waiting for her response, he strode out of Muldoon's Bar.

EPILOGUE

CORD BUFFETT —
CALIFORNIA — ALMOST A
YEAR LATER

His bear bounded through the woods, moving as fast as his hulking size would allow. Mouth open, the myriad scents filtering through his senses carried the unwelcome tang of motor oil and fuel. Cord clacked his teeth together, displeased his private sanctuary was about to be invaded.

Giving up his hunt, he made his way back to his mountain home, falling into step with his brother's shiny red and black '69 Mustang Mach 1. While Cord dodged around trees, skirted stumps, and bypassed bushes, Benny was forced to rein in the horsepower of his V8 engine on the rough, narrow track of Cord's private driveway. Without knowing it was a race, Benny reached the cabin first.

Cord burst into the manicured garden as the passenger door of Benny's car swung shut.

A scream rent the air, rupturing Cord's ears. He roared, bolting forward to challenge the woman disturbing his peace.

Benny's hands clenched. "What the Hell, Cord? Are you trying to give my wife a heart attack?"

"Cord?" Elena's voice shook. Her startled eyes unblinking, she gaped at the giant Kodiak.

Shifting back to his human form, Cord approached Benny. "Where the Hell have you been? I expected you six months ago."

Elena squealed, her hands slapping over her eyes, cracking her fingers just enough to peak at the naked form of her brother-in-law.

Benny grimaced, and pulled Elena into his arms, pressing her head against his chest to block the view. "Bro, put some bloody clothes on, I don't need you flaunting your junk in front of my wife."

Cord laughed and made his way to the front door. "I wasn't expecting company, otherwise I would have been ready for you. Like I said, you were supposed to be back six months ago." Cord disappeared into the shadowy depths of his house, leaving the door ajar for Benny and Elena to follow.

He headed to the bedroom, where he grabbed the grey sweatpants off the bed, and a fresh T-shirt from the drawer. Dressing quickly, he padded to the living area, hearing

Elena's hushed whisper before he reached the end of the hallway.

"Why didn't you tell me your brother was a shifter?"

"Honestly, Sweetpea, it wasn't my secret to tell, otherwise I would have done. I tell you everything else."

Cord rounded the corner to see Elena perched on the edge of his oversized leather sectional, Benny crouched at her feet, trying to get her to look at him. Instead, her gaze was fixed firmly on the wall of windows overlooking the rambling garden leading into the overgrown forest of Cord's land.

He followed her line of sight, and lopsided grin crept onto his face when he spotted it. Near the arch of cottonwood which created a natural gateway into the forest, a tail flicked back and forth in the air.

He entered the room and, at his most urbane, said, "I'm the same man you've always known, Ellie. There's just a hidden extra, a bonus if you like, that's all." Cord slid open the patio door, his gaze locking onto a pair of glowing orbs deep in the cover of the cottonwood. He crooked a finger, beckoning her to him.

"Not sure there's anything left to learn about you, after your little flash," Elena scoffed, her eyes raking his body.

"Little?" choked Cord.

Elena cleared her throat. "Ok, not so little—"

"Oi," Benny huffed, pinching Elena's thigh.

"Oh. My. God." Elena scrambled onto the top of the couch, shoving Benny in front of her. "Shut the door, Cord, now. There's a giant bloody cat stalking you."

The heavy weight of the leopard winding against the back of Cord's legs nearly knocked him off his feet. "I acquired a house cat while you were taking an *unauthorised*, extended honeymoon."

Her tail whipped him, slapping his ass with a hard thwack, wicked teeth exposed with her grumble annoyance.

"Careful, kitten," warned Cord. Sinuously, she sidled past him, hackles up.

Elena shoved Benny in front of her again, but her feet slipped on the leather cushion, and she would have fallen if not for her death grip on her husband.

The leopard disappeared down the hallway to the bedroom, breaking the spell holding Benny frozen. Stupefied, he whirled around to gape at his brother.

"What?" He pointed at the hallway. "You want to explain the freaking zoo animal wandering your house at will?"

Cord shut the door, his face alight with silent laughter. "House cat, not a zoo animal. Get it right, Benny boy."

"House cat? House cat?" Stevie's voice rose an octave with every word. She reappeared at the corner of the hall, smoothing her silk kaftan over her thighs. "Call me a house cat again, and I'll skin you for a rug."

Benny reeled around to his wife when he heard her collapse on the sofa behind him. She was still conscious, her blue eyes on the other woman in the room.

Elena started to giggle, her nervous chortle blooming into a belly-aching guffaw. "She's...a...noth...er...shif...ter," she gasped out between her mirth.

"Skin me for a rug?" Cord shook his head, a smile playing at his mouth. "Come here, kitten. Let me introduce you to my baby brother, Benny, and his wife, Elena."

Stevie crossed the room, her bare feet silent on the polished wood of the floor. She allowed Cord to press her against his hard body and drape an arm over her shoulders. "It's a pleasure to meet you, Benny, Elena."

"Guys, this is my mate, Stevie."

"Mate?" Benny struggled to speak.

Elena smacked his arm with the back of her hand. "That's shifter for wife." She raised her brows at Cord and Stevie, "Right?"

Cord looked down at Stevie, her big eyes shone with her inner cat's radiance when she met his gaze. His heart thudded. She was his everything, had snuck into every corner of his heart and stolen his breath. She had given his life new meaning. Eradicated the pain of his mother's loss and changed his focus. *Was Stevie his wife?* "Yeah," he husked.

He lifted his head. "If you pair hadn't stayed away twice as long, gallivanting around the world like a pair of lovesick doves, you'd have known what's been going on."

Benny dropped back into the sofa, shuffling until Elena was his arms. "Oh? And just what *is* going on?"

Cord sat on the smaller love seat set at an angle from the large sofa, and tucked Stevie onto his lap. "I'm resigning from the board of Buffett Property Group. I'll be suggesting you take my place as CEO."

Benny lunged forward, shoving Elena away. "What? No. You can't. The company, it's your life, it's all you've ever talked about."

Cord shrugged, the back of his fingers stroking Stevie's arm. "Maybe, once a upon a time, but not anymore. The tribe needs me more and, well, I think that's where my time would be better spent."

"What tribe?" Benny' glowered. "You don't mean that bloody bear pack who haunted Mom, do you?"

With a sigh, Cord nodded. "It was all a lie. Mom was the true mate of the Torben alpha. It's a long story, but if you've the time I'll tell it."

Elena tweaked Benny's shirt, encouraging him to settle back on the sofa, and squeezed his thigh. "We're listening, Cord," she said, not taking her eyes from her husband, "Aren't we, Ben?".

Cord twirled the glass of Macallan in his hand. Beside him, Benny mirrored his actions. It had been a long afternoon, drawing into the dark of evening, sharing so much information with his brother.

"You're sure then?" Benny twisted to look at Cord, his eyes a little glazed from the Scotch he had consumed.

Cord nodded. "I am. I need to be in Pineville. I need to lead the Torben people, rebuild the tribe's stability after so many years of being exploited by a narcissistic witch."

Benny chugged back his last mouthful of Scotch. "Good." He slammed down the glass. "It's what Mom wanted for you."

"What?" Cord frowned and spun on his stool to face Benny. "What do you mean?"

"She always regretted you didn't grow up with shifters," Benny disclosed. "She recognised a strength in you which equalled the man who — well — you know, made you. She just wasn't brave enough to confront her fears and take you back there."

"She told you this?"

Benny's eyes slid closed, his body starting to slump against the edge of the bar where they sat. "Nope, not me directly. I heard Mom and Dad talking about it. It was one of those nights when you went all bear on us and stormed out in a huff."

Cord grunted, "Which one? There were many of those nights when I was growing up."

"S-actly," Benny slurred. "You're a good brother, Cord, but you have one mean-ass temper on you."

Stevie snorted from her place curled up by the fire on the other side of the room.

Cord contemplated her, his dark eyes brooding.

A sheet of lightening severed the sky, illuminating the Angeles National Forest and silhouetting Elena standing at the window.

"What will you do with this place when you move to Oregon?" Elena asked before the thunder rolled around the cabin.

Cord looked through the highest corner of the window, trying to see beyond the inky blackness of a moonless night. "It's yours if you want it, providing Stevie and I are welcome to stay when we come back to California for a visit."

Elena's face softened into a serene smile. "I've always loved this place."

"So did Mom," murmured Cord. He placed his tumbler, still half full of Scotch, on the bar. Standing, he stretched, then scooped up Benny before he tumbled off his perch. His brother snored against his arm while Cord manoeuvred him to the sofa. "He never could hold his liquor," he chuckled, laying Benny on the cushions.

"We'll make new memories, my alpha," whispered Stevie, stepping into Cord's waiting arms. She rested her head on his chest, watching the magnificence of the storm scudding across the obsidian sky.

"Yeah, kitten, we will." He dropped a kiss on the top of her head, squeezing her shoulder three times. Stevie challenged him every day, but he wouldn't have it any other way. Never had his world felt so right, so balanced, so... happy. Inwardly, he rolled his eyes at his whimsy but knew, without a shadow of a doubt, as long as he had Stevie by his side, his anchor in the storm, he could do anything. Creating new memories were the least of it.

She traced a finger against his side, drawing letters, one over the other. When she poked him with a full stop, her head tilted upwards.

He looked down, meeting her fathomless gaze, Elena and Benny forgotten.

"I love you," she mouthed.

Cord's heart thumped in his chest. "I love you, too, kitten."

Silent messages winged between them, reaffirming a bond already indissoluble.

With a shared smile, as one, they faced the window, captivated by the incredible power of mother nature.

The End

Want to know how Magda claimed her very own alpha bear?

Keep reading to find the bonus story 'Her Desired Bear'.

If you enjoyed my book, don't forget to check out the others in the collection.

Return to Blackcreek by Quell T. Fox -

https://books2read.com/returntoblackcreek

Bear With Me by TJ Bell -

https://www.amazon.com/dp/B0BGKGXZQR

Claiming Emma by Leeah Taylor -

https://www.amazon.com/dp/B0BGK9LYVD

For the Good of the Clan by Lucille Yates -

https://books2read.com/u/boyyj0

Unexpected Mate by Morgan Meyer -

https://www.amazon.com/dp/B0BGVBY6M7

HER

DESIRED

BEAR

CHAPTER ONE

The forest floor was damp under Magda's knees while she harvested the roots she needed, the chill seep of yesterday's rain through her dress, adding to her discomfort.

The ground trembled beneath her. The pleasant songs of nature stopped with an unpleasant squawk when chirping birds flew away from incoming danger.

Magda dropped her small trowel to spear both hands into the mulch and upturned dirt, connecting herself with the earth. Eyes closed, she concentrated on the tremors and, reading the land, calculated the direction of the disturbance. She was a human in shifter territory. It wasn't any major secret that shifters existed, although for the most part, humanity chose not to acknowledge the fact. Magda didn't ignore them. She was fascinated by their sheer animal magnetism, their power.

Opening her eyes, she tilted her head, but her enjoyment of the rising sun's gentle caress was fleeting.

Two bears lumbered around the tall trees, barrelling through shrubbery as though it didn't exist.

With a roar, the larger of the pair took a swipe at its companion. A back leg was caught in a giant paw and yanked out from under the smaller beast.

Magda trembled with the impact when the dirty brown bear face planted the mud. Being here could put her in grave danger. The ground vibrated under the violent pounding of paws.

Fascinated by the raw beauty and sheer power of the two brawling bears, Magda watched, her breath trapped in her throat, lower lip pinned between her teeth.

Her stomach tightened, muscles clenched in nervous anticipation watching the two creatures duel with tooth and claw. Blood splattered to the ground with one particularly vicious bite to the smaller bear's shoulder.

Despite his bravado, and the stoic fight he put up, eventually, the juvenile bear gave up. His body went lax and, angling his head to bare the vulnerable curve of his neck, he submitted to the giant kodiak.

Magda's breath tumbled out of her mouth only to be sucked back in through her nose, *would the larger beast accept the submission or land a death blow*?

The wickedly long teeth, brushed pink with blood, glistened in the early morning light, before snapping shut mere inches from the throat of the prone beast.

Lip quivering with the release of a long, low growl, the victor communicated his will to the loser.

Another faltering breath released from Magda's mouth when the air shimmered. Fur faded from the defeated creature who convulsed and diminished until a man cowered under the immense paws of the bear towering over him.

On his hind legs, the triumphant bear stood almost eight feet high. The air shimmered once more, the beast's immense proportions barely changing when it assumed the form of a human male.

Feeling her bottom lip throbbing, Magda ran her tongue over the maligned flesh and squirmed, knees burrowing into the soft, mulched forest floor.

Every solid plane of his body was sculpted into pure muscle. A thick head of brown curls tempted her fingers. She flexed them in the dirt, imagining the silken softness of his locks. He was her idea of perfection.

"Scamper back where you came from, cub." His voice, a deep, gravelly rumble rode the breeze to reverberate through her core. "The Torben tribe has no place for wannabe alphas."

The other male, equally naked, yet somehow not nearly as impressive in physique or looks, scrambled to his feet, and legged it. He looked back to check he wasn't being pursued before slamming into a tree. Bouncing off the unforgiving trunk, he shook his head, adjusted his path, and sprinted away.

Magda lost interest in the retreat of the humiliated male and turned to regard the one who had captured her attention.

His face was dark and broody whilst he concentrated on the banished bear. Thick arms, corded with ropey muscles, stiffened when he folded them across his chest. A thrum, like the sound of distant thunder, grumbled out of the disapproving slash of his mouth.

Magda kneaded the dirt, anchoring herself in place resisting the urge to stand. She quashed the desire to trace every inch of his rippled torso or sweep her hands over his narrow hips. It was not necessary to feel the thickness of his legs to know every part of him would be equally large and heavy.

She wanted him.

No.

She didn't want him.

She *needed* him.

Need was so much more than want. Need enforced the intention, and intention was what created the power to shape her world and what she coveted from it.

Ensnared by his dominating presence, Magda remained rooted to the spot beneath the giant oak, surrounded by the wildflowers she had been carefully harvesting. She studied the shifter male as intently as he studied the man, he had driven out. She committed everything she could see of him — and there wasn't much she *couldn't* see — to memory.

After what seemed a lifetime, he moved, unfolding his arms to rest his hands on his hips, fingers splayed.

"You know this is shifter territory, woman. Humans are not supposed to be here." He swivelled around, fixing her with a gaze so intense, Magda felt as though she was drowning in his dark eyes.

"I..." Her voice cracked in a dry throat. Swallowing in a futile attempt to lubricate her vocal cords, she husked, "I only wanted these roots. It's a rare plant, I haven't found it elsewhere."

His chin jutted forward; head canted in response. "Why do you want the roots?"

Magda tried to smile, fluttering her lashes for a moment, delaying her answer. No one understood her affinity with nature, her love for the potency of botany.

"I... I'm a botanist, I have a small plot on the edge of Pineville. I cultivate rare and endangered plants and sell the more common species online."

"Why? Why would you do that?"

His engaging her in conversation settled Magda. Relaxing, she smiled unreservedly. "Not everyone has access to nature, and there are those who enjoy having plants around them. So I help by selling seedlings, or sometimes just the bulbs, seeds, or root stock."

He frowned, and stepped closer. "You're charging for plants you have taken from shifter land?"

Her smile faltered, unease curling in her belly again. "No," she was grateful her reply was strong and clear. "These are for my own personal collection, my pleasure. Everything I sell comes from plants I grow myself, from cuttings or seeds sourced from human lands."

He stalked towards her, resolve in every step.

"You are on tribe lands, a human trespassing on shifter territory. You are taking what doesn't belong to you."

Despite the danger written across his handsome features, there was a note in his voice that teased her.

Holding her own, she remained kneeling, hands still half-buried in the earth. She flexed her fingers, once. Twice. Three times.

"What are you going to do? Eat me?" Her question sounded sassy even to her own ears.

He stopped inches from her, his bulk blocking out the sun, he looked down at her.

"I just might." His grin wicked, light glinted in his eyes. He reached down, fingers digging into her skin, to grip her shoulders and haul her upright.

Magda couldn't prevent a squeal, or the dirt that clung to her fingers when she grabbed his arms to steady herself, trembling under his scrutiny.

His lip curled back in a strange mix of smirk and snarl, revealing a flash of white teeth. Warmth radiated across her shoulder when his meaty fingers trailed down her arm. Sparks of energy zinged through her body at the promise of his touch. When he reached her hip, his fist bunched into the light cotton of her dress, tugging at the material, drawing it up until he held the hem in his hand. In one swift motion, the material slithered over her head and floated to the ground.

The lazy morning breeze swirled across her bare flesh, pebbling her exposed nipples to hard points, and cooling her heated body. Magda tilted her chin, daring the alpha to chastise her lack of underwear. She didn't care, comfortable in her own skin.

The bear of a man growled deep in his chest as he surveyed her naked form, his fingers explored until, with bruising intensity, he clamped his hands around her waist.

Effortlessly, he lifted her, and she hovered above him, riveted by the hunger in his eyes, her back scraped against a tree.

"Open your legs, woman," he snarled.

Magda grinned, drawing up her legs to slide one foot, and then the other over his shoulders. Her head fell back, hair snagging in the bark when his tongue stabbed at her core. His rough stubble scratched the tender flesh of her thigh.

CHAPTER TWO

Magda flipped down the sun visor to check her pale reflection in the mirror. Her eyes seemed brighter than usual, although whether from the new eyeliner framing them, or from her encounter in the woods, she wasn't sure. Her hair required a little teasing to fix the curls before she uncapped her lipstick to smooth the ruby red matte across her full lips. Rolling them in then out before sucking her finger to remove any excess that might mark her teeth, she smacked a kiss at the mirror, confident she looked perfect.

Her journal lay open on the passenger seat, the pen caught in the spiral binder. She only needed to write her intention of the day once more to cement its power. Closing her eyes, she focused on what she wanted, *who* she wanted then focused her gaze on the page and wrote down her intention.

The closer she got to being ready to enter Muldoon's, the stronger she felt. The small perfume bottle was the last step; one spritz to the base of her throat, the second and third on her wrists before dropping the glass bottle into her clutch next to the packet of caraway seeds.

Three deep breaths infused her senses with the powerful, yet subtle aroma of rose, cinnamon, and gardenia. Satisfied, she opened her car door and stepped out.

Muldoon's was a bar straddling the edge of Pineville. Three quarters of the building was on the shifter side of the dividing line which skimmed ten percent of the original township away from human territory and into shifter control. Muldoon himself, was a bear-shifter and his mate had been human until he claimed her. The Muldoons and their bar had become a natural buffer between the humans and shifters.

The bar itself was a neutral zone, a place where the local government officials could meet with the shifters if it proved necessary to discuss matters which impacted everyone. It had happened twice in the fifty or more years since the shifter council and human governing officials in the State of Oregon had reached the accord which divided the town.

Pineville was the only border town in the State with a bar that served both shifters and humans. While there were only four cars parked in front of the building on the human side of Pineville, the bar would have plenty of patrons.

There were few shifters in the United States who associated with humans, and even less humans who would have anything to do with shifters. In fact, a large proportion of American citizens walked around blindly refusing to accept shifters existed.

Magda knew they existed, was fascinated by them. Drawn to the allure of unknown power and animal magnetism, she had made her home as close as possible to the border, choosing Pineville *because* of Muldoon's bar.

She had acknowledged it was destiny for her to be here when the realtor showed her the rentals in town. The third house she had been shown was 'the one'.

The third house, on the third street, on a three-acre block only three miles from the shifter border.

She didn't even worry that the house required more work than the others she had seen, the power of three cemented her intentions.

Flicking her hair over her shoulder, while smoothing her rear to ensure her little black dress wasn't rumpled, Magda strutted across the parking lot to the entrance of the bar. Her three-inch stiletto heels struck the asphalt in a confident tattoo — the red of the suede, the perfect match to the red belt cinching her narrow waist.

All heads turned; gazes locked on her when she stepped inside the dimly lit log cabin-style interior, prompting her to straighten her shoulders just enough to lift her chest.

The low neckline of her dress displayed the rose quartz crystal — hanging from a fine three-strand plaited leather thong and nestled against her cleavage — to perfection. She was dressed to seduce, and a quick scan, showed her target already seated at the bar.

Magda allowed her gaze to glide up the strong planes of his back, barely covered by the thin cotton of his t-shirt. His hair was messy, the locks curling over his broad shoulders. Then she saw them. The dark, brooding eyes of a dominant alpha. He was looking in the mirror hanging behind the bar... watching her.

Curving one corner of her mouth in the smile she had practised all evening, Magda sashayed across the timber boards, her eyes fixed on him, chanting inwardly, '*He will be mine. He will be mine. He will be mine.*'

He tried to hide his cocky smirk behind his beer glass, but she saw the approval in the twist of his lips not yet hidden by the thickening beard covering the lower half of his face.

He hadn't complained about her appearance that morning, when he had hauled her from the dirt and pinned her against the oak tree, stripping away her organic cotton tie dye summer dress to reveal she wore nothing else. Even so, Magda knew, the femme fatale she presented now, little black dress, red pumps and red belt was far more attractive.

She reached the bar. Averting her gaze from his reflection, while somehow feeling the scorching touch of his eyes, she perched on the leather stool next to his. Crossing one leg over the other, she shortened the length of her dress which emphasised the curve of her thigh. Her heart beat a steady rhythm, belying the knot of nerves pulsing low in her belly.

She didn't just want this man to want her.

She *needed* him to *need* her.

She could feel his magnetism. He leaned in and whispered in her ear. "Have you come to steal more roots from lands you have no business being on, woman?"

Magda turned, her voluptuous breasts pushing up towards his face. Satisfaction curled in her chest, when his eyes dropped to stare at her, his nostrils flaring when he inhaled her scent.

She trailed one red painted nail along his bearded jaw, then, sliding it under his chin, tilted his head upwards with minimal pressure. Arching a manicured brow, she held his stare.

"Who said I needed to steal anything, Alpha?"

Her thumb grazed the cleft obscured by the bristly stubble. With a quick smile she dropped her hand from his face and, swinging around on her seat, almost dismissing him, called for the bartender.

"A bottle of red wine and two glasses," she ordered, before looking askance at the giant beside her. "Are you up for a little treat?"

His eyes narrowed. "What are you up to, woman?"

Her cheeks tightened with her smile, challenging him with her eyes. "You showed me so much... generosity this morning, let me show you my gratitude now."

About to place her clutch on the bar, she hesitated, and dropped it back on her lap. It clicked open between her fingers easily, and she withdrew the little sachet of caraway seeds.

"I told you I grow and sell plants but, did you know, they are not just pretty to look at? They make food and drink taste really good."

He took the little cloth packet from her, his fingers hot against her skin when he touched her. "What do you have here?"

Two glasses and an opened bottle of red wine appeared between them.

"Please pour the wine, it will breathe better in the glasses," she asked the barman, then faced the bear, her small hand barely circled the fingers holding her tiny pouch. Her breathing quickened at the memory of those enormous hands gripping her waist to hold her high so expertly.

"They are only a simple herb seed; they just add a little... depth to the wine, to... enhance the evening." Deliberately, she fluttered her hand towards the tips of his fingers, watching his pupils dilate. The seed packet fell into her grasp at her gentle tug.

Untying the drawstring, she opened the bag and tipped some out into her cupped palm. Carefully, she counted out seven seeds and, one by one, dropped them into her glass. Dipping her middle finger into her wine she stirred the contents... one... two... three times. Removing her finger, she placed it in her mouth and, closing her red lips around the digit, made eye contact, then sucked the wine off slowly, pulling her finger out with a soft pop.

"Will you join me, Alpha?" Her invitation dared him.

With a half growl, he answered her challenge. "Why not."

Tearing her gaze away, she repeated the process of counting out seven seeds and tipped them into his wine.

CHAPTER THREE

A smile curved Magda's lips upon waking. Ryan Jones, alpha bear of the Torben tribe was a god among men. Magda stretched out in her bed, the sheets sliding across her skin. She was still a little uncomfortable from the night's activities, but he was worth every sore muscle. Magda neither knew nor cared whether she was under the influence of the caraway seeds, her body yearned for more of the same. Rolling over, she reached across cold sheets in search of her lover.

She didn't find him. A frown marring her brow, she opened her eyes to find her bed and her room devoid of the Herculean male.

Fingers curling into the sheets, Magda sat up, resisting the urge to scream. Instead, she closed her eyes, breathed deeply to the count of three, then exhaled in the same manner. Repeating the ritual twice more centred her again.

She could feel the residual headiness of the aphrodisiac the pair had drunk. The wine and caraway continued to heighten her physical senses, *so why had her bear vanished?*

Her *bear*. Perhaps she had failed to account for the fact, he was a shifter. His body may have already expelled the effects.

Flinging back the red silk sheet, Magda swung her legs over the side of the mattress and stood up. A groan bubbled out when she moved, feeling the chaffed skin between her thighs, and the ache which follows unexpected exercise.

"Still worth it." She caught sight of herself in the full-length mirror in the corner. The purplish prints on her hips evoking the image of massive hands holding her in place for his punishing rhythm. Her pussy throbbed at the memory of his thick cock filling every inch of her, pounding against her cervix; he had fucked her with uncontrolled passion.

It had been a fine line between pain and pleasure, and she had savoured every minute of it. She wanted him again, needed to feel his cock while he stretched her womanhood, teased the sensitive flesh of her pussy, and claimed every inch of her body. She wanted to be used by him. Needed his power whilst he slaked his own thirst for sex with her body.

She wanted him.

No.

She *needed* him. For more than just one night.

The intention of her desires cemented in place she strode across to her dresser, opened the drawer, and withdrew a new journal and pen.

On a pristine page, she set down her words, reinforcing her purpose by committing her affirmation to paper.

I will have Ryan Jones, my alpha bear, for all my life

I will have Ryan Jones, my alpha bear, for all my life

She kept writing until she had repeated it ten times, the black ink in stark contrast with the snowy whiteness of the page. Tensing her toes against the beautiful, smooth wood floor, she grounded herself. She needed to be calm and logical before she made her next move for the alpha bear.

She craved him. She needed him to yearn for her. Beyond one night tumbling together. She wanted him for life. She had experienced his strength, touched his power, and she ached for, no... *needed* more.

Magda was confident she could break through the stigma of human and shifter pairings. Certain she would bring him to his knees until he was begging for her, succumbing to wild abandonment in his desire to please her.

The vision of him — bending over her toes to explore her feet and her legs with his lips as he worshipped her body and begged for her heart — rekindled the flame.

Shaking off the heat crawling across her skin and pooling at her core, Magda broke from the trance before she was lost to it.

Tea.

Tea fixed so many ills and soothed the mind. On her way out of the bedroom, she grabbed her silk kaftan from the back of the chair. Slipping it over her body, she made her way downstairs, already planning what herbs and spices to blend for her tea when she entered the kitchen.

Opening the door of her wood-fire stove, she was pleased to see the red glow of the night log. The wood had reduced to charcoal, but the embers meant only kindling and a larger branch were required to stoke the stove back to life.

Once the fire was laid, she adjusted the vents for the appropriate air draw, then lifted the cover of the hot plate to put the kettle on.

Humming her meditations, she busied herself by adding a pinch of peppermint, ginger, and clove powder to her favourite mug, ready to brew a good, healing tea. She needed her strength to keep her bear happy.

When the kettle whistled, she poured hot water over the spices and allowed the tea to steep, while she sat at the ash-wood table to make up three miniature cloth spell packets.

Magda required something more permanent for Ryan. Something that could work around the clock on her bear since the caraway in wine only lasted until his shifter blood metabolised the alcohol along with her love potion.

Meadowsweet.

It would be beneficial to increase the potency of her concoctions. Leaving the table, she unlocked the back door and stepped outside. The early morning sun bathed the riot of plants in its warm glow and sank into her body. Inhaling the myriad scents, Magda smiled. This was her sanctuary. Every plant she grew had a purpose, a place in her garden.

Flowers were starting to unfurl after being closed for the night, and the colour of the blooms were creeping into her space. July was a good time of year to harvest meadowsweet; its flowers were in bud, but not yet turned to cotton candy fluff. It stood tall at the bottom of the garden, its roots reaching deep into the damp ground edging the little creek she had encouraged to meander through the lower portion of her plot of land for those plants and herbs which flourished in wet ground.

Thanking the universe for the bountiful harvest, Magda snipped a stem of meadowsweet between the sharp curve of her thumb nail and index finger. Brushing her face with the creamy white flower head, she inhaled the sweet fragrance and strolled indoors.

Magda deposited the meadowsweet on the table, which doubled as her workbench and daily altar.

Resuming her seat, she peeked into her mug of tea. Happy it was steeped to her liking, Magda took a sip. It was a balm to her soul, and she knew her body would heal.

Picking up her pencil, she began to jot down the potential ingredients for the spell packet, on her scrap pad.

Apple

Balm of Gilead

Basil

Caraway

Coriander

Dill

Dragon's Blood

Ginseng

Honeysuckle

Lemon

Lemon Verbena

Lilac

Linden

Marigold

Marjoram

Mint

Myrtle

Orange peel

Orris Root

Patchouli

Rose

Rosemary

Valerian

Vanilla

Vervain

Violet

Yarrow

Dropping her pencil, she looked at the note pad. Unwittingly, she had used the power of three. Her ingredients bundled in multiples of three. She had plenty of choice.

Unconsciously, Magda tapped out a three-beat rhythm on the table's surface and studied her list, while drinking her tea.

Mug cradled in one hand, she picked up the pencil again and circled her preferred choice of nine herbs currently in season or already prepared in her herb room.

"I need honeysuckle, jasmine, and lovage as well," she said to the empty room, planning her own charm, and the perfume she would wear the next time she approached Ryan.

Her tea finished, Magda set about filling her spell sachets; three measures of each ingredient. Each bag was threaded with three strands of red, black, and gold string, then tied closed in an intricate three knot pattern. Standing, she touched the packets on the table. One. Two. Three. One. Two. Three. One. Two. Three.

Satisfied with her work and the ritual, Magda headed upstairs to enjoy a hot soak in a cowslip milk bath. She had to find Ryan soon, secrete her packets into his car, his workspace and, if possible, his bed. She required the consistent influence of her herbs to ensure she captured her desired bear's undivided attention.

CHAPTER FOUR

Not only was Ryan Jones the alpha of the Torben bear tribe but also, he was a blacksmith. He used his natural strength and size to his advantage. Bearing in mind, shifters preferred not to do business with humans, and vice versa, Magda was unsure what would keep a blacksmith busy in the modern world.

She was pleasantly surprised when she pulled through the intricate, wrought-iron gates of Torben Smithworks. The courtyard was flagged with pale sandstone. Old fashioned wagon wheels marked out several parking spaces along one side of the L shaped building. The other side was decorated with perfect displays of wrought-iron work and wine barrel planters. The riot of flowers cascading from the plants attracted plenty of bees, giving the courtyard the soft hum of industry.

Magda pulled her vehicle in beside the huge black truck, her lips quirked in triumph when she spotted the reserved name plate worked into the wheel in front of the truck.

Ryan Jones

Head blacksmith

The window was down on the driver's side, making Magda wonder whether it was rank arrogance on the part of her bear was not worried about the vehicle being stolen, or whether there were security cameras. Scrutinising the decor on the sandstone façade of the large building Magda searched for a camera. Not seeing one prompted her to retrieve the first spell packet from her bag.

After another surreptitious glance around and she perched on the running board of the bear's truck and leaned through the window. Her fingers rubbed across the cloth in her hand, the intention of her spell recited in her mind, her affirmation clear when she stated her intention while she reached through the driver's side of the car. Carefully, she squeezed the spell packet between the seat and the back rest, so it was as close to the driver as possible.

Sighing in relief, she stepped back onto the sandstone flags.

Smoothing her cotton sundress, Magda used the tinted rear windows of the big black truck to preen herself. Blowing her reflection a kiss, she hitched the strap of her bag higher on her shoulder and strutted across the courtyard into Torben Smithworks.

The front door slid open at her approach, and a blast of artificially chilled air flowed over her body when she entered, pebbling her nipples under the thin dress. Her shoulders straightened and she pushed out her chest under the curious gaze of the older man sitting at the sales desk. Her self-assurance, a shield, she swept across the immaculate tiled floor like she owned the place.

"I'm here to see Ryan."

His expression one of distaste, the man's eyes narrowed to rake over her body. "Alpha has no time for shiftless tra-" he corrected himself with a cough, "humans."

Belly tightening, and fingers bunching into a fist, Magda hardened her gaze while pasting a smile on her face, "He has all the time in the world for me," *stupid, old bear* she added in her head. "Is he out the back?"

Without waiting for a response, she turned towards the distant ring of hammering metal, and with a sway of her hips, drew in every strand of positive energy from the world. Mentally, she cloaked herself in confidence and, when she passed a mirror mounted on a pillar, saw her sex appeal in her loose curls, red lips, curvy body, and summery dress. The red roses on crisp white cotton emphasised her desire. She was here to seduce and capture the heart of her alpha bear.

A chair scraped across the floor behind her, "Hey, shiftless! You can't be here."

Throwing her hands up she spun around, indicating the rich display of metalwork across the showroom. "Er, hello. This is a showroom, a place of business. Open to the public." Finishing her rotation, she headed to the large, medieval-style double doors, at the rear of the display room, the rough-hewn wood branded with the letters **f o r g**

e. The sound of hammering increased the closer she got. The intricate beauty of the wrought-iron fence sections, staircases, hinges, and posts exhibited for customers to browse amongst was almost lost on her; she zeroed in on her target.

I will have my alpha bear.

I will have my alpha bear.

I will have my alpha bear.

The internal mantra was all that kept her from losing her temper at the racist old man shuffling after her.

"This is a shifter business, on shifter lands. Weak, useless humans aren't welcome here."

Gritting her teeth to hold back her own choice words, Magda reached for the huge black ring, which served as a door handle. Expecting such a large door to be heavy, she exerted considerable force into lifting the handle. It moved so smoothly, she nearly toppled off her feet when the door swung open.

Heat blasted her skin. A sharp contrast with the conditioned air behind her. Instantly, sweat beaded on her upper lip and her brow grew damp. The smell of scorched metal tickled her sinuses, immediately forgotten at the view before her.

"You can't go in there. That's private space not even shifter public can go in there." The man's voice dropped to an aggrieved muttering, but she still heard him abusing her under his breath, "Stupid, lowly, soul-deprived human bitch, thinks she can paint on her slut face and make the alpha dance her tune."

Rolling her eyes at the persistent droning of the bigoted old bear, Magda pivoted on her heel and shoved the door closed. There was a heavy beam style latch, which she slotted in place across the doors to keep the old fool out.

The rhythmic clanging of the blacksmith's hammer disguised the heavy clunk of the beam and granted Magda the leisure of relishing the view.

Ryan's jeans were slung low over his hips, and he wore leather chaps around his legs which framed his tight ass while protecting the denim from the hot slag sparking off the glowing red metal being thumped against the anvil. The bare muscles of Ryan's back rippled with every strike. His tanned skin, smudged with the dirt of his trade, was running in intriguing patterns with the sweat gliding down his body.

Tongue darting out to moisten dry lips, Magda's core tightened at the sheer masculinity of the giant bear of a man. Even the pounding on the door behind her couldn't dampen her exhilaration as she watched Ryan wield his hammer.

He straightened, and lifted the glowing metal in his massive tongs, turning it one way then the other before plunging it into a vat of water next to the anvil.

Steam billowed up from the water's bubbling surface, momentarily obscuring her view.

Without the addictive vision, she scanned the rest of the workshop. A grin tugged at the corner of her mouth when she spotted the battered leather jacket hanging over the back of a chair to her right. It was the same coat he had worn the previous night. The supple feel of the aged leather when she had helped him out of it, along with the frayed cuffs, indicated the coat was worn often, and probably a favourite piece of clothing.

Stepping closer to the chair, Magda looked across to the steam dissipating from around Ryan. He was still absorbed in his work. Dropping into the chair, Magda fished out the second spell packet. Eyes firmly fixed on the blacksmith, she ran her hand over the silky lining of the jacket until she found a small, inner pocket in which to slip her little sachet. Her thumb circled over the barely definable bulge of the jacket's lining three times, repeating the intention of her spell in her mind, before she withdrew her hand.

She had propped her elbow on the back of the chair and was resting her chin on her palm when Ryan spotted her.

His face, smudged with soot from the fire, creased into a frown before one eyebrow arced. He dropped his hammer onto the anvil with a clunk that rang through the workroom before he strode towards her. His steps were slow, measured. A predator stalking his prey.

Magda shifted on the chair and, rubbing her thighs together, sought to relieve some of the pressure this beast of a man created within her.

"Woman. There are no plants to steal here. No alcohol to drink either come to think of it."

Her laughter was soft, as she gave him her best smile. "Oh, Alpha, there is so much more to this life than plants or alcohol. You left my bed too soon to understand just what you are being offered."

He towered over her, one hand on the bench behind her, the other gripping the chair back near her elbow. His nose was inches from hers. Nostrils flared; he sucked in a deep breath. The heat of the room had raised her body temperature, and the air around them was infused with her perfume. Ryan's eyes glazed a little as the jasmine and honeysuckle took effect on his senses.

His voice rumbled at her, breath holding the faint aroma of coffee. "I don't make a habit of staying in bed with the women I rut. Or rutting them more than once, for that matter."

Cupping his stubbled jaw, Magda gaze darted over every nuance of his face. Her red painted thumb nail stood out against his smudged skin; she grazed it along his full lower lip.

"Those other women you...err... rutted before me... merely good practice. Now, you have something better."

He didn't look convinced. "Such as?"

Magda slipped her foot out of her sandal, running her toes up his inseam, aiming for the hardness that filled his jeans. "A reason to spend more time in your bed. Me."

Ryan's growl came from somewhere deep within him, until it pulsed through her foot and tingled up her leg. His grin was wicked, he hauled her flush to his body, mouth descending on the curve of her neck and shoulder. His hand tracked up her thigh, lifting her dress until his fingers swept across the bare skin of her hip, his approval for her lack of underwear clear when his fingers dug deeper into her flesh.

She shivered. His stubble, the antithesis of the wet slide of his tongue when he lapped at her throat. Her dress stuck to his damp flesh, her hands slipping over the thick sheen of sweat coating his shoulders, she clawed to get closer.

The heat of the forge faded. He carried her away, his mouth latched onto her neck, his grip unyielding.

Magda gasped, "Where are we going?"

The pressure of his teeth on her delicate skin bordered on painful, yet so pleasurable, she was ready to cum in his arms before he even touched her pussy.

He let go and grazed his nose up her neck to nuzzle behind her ear. "You should be careful what you wish for little witch. I have an apartment upstairs. You wanted in my bed? Well, I'm going to punish that tight little pussy of yours when I pound you into my bed."

Magda quivered in anticipation, her core convulsed with desire, her nipples puckered against his hard chest. The heavy fall of his steps changed when they clanged against something metal. She felt them ascending, and glimpsed the elaborate ironwork of a spiral staircase over his shoulder. She couldn't keep count of the steps because his mouth nibbled at her neck, teasing her with the bite she wanted most of all. Yet he never broke her skin.

Ryan reached the top of the stairs, his booted feet stomped across a mezzanine landing until a door banged open. His teeth relinquished her neck, he raised his head, letting her slither down his muscled chest until she was wobbling on her feet. He stepped back, to tap her nose with the tip of his right index finger.

"Strip, witch. I'll be back in a moment."

She watched him walk away, his muscles undulating across his torso. He looked back.

"If you aren't ready for me, I will punish you," he said disappearing through another door.

Mouth dry, Magda struggled to swallow, *dare she test his level of dominance?* Tossing her bag on to the pile of laundry in front of her, deciding compliance was the best course of action to get what she wanted at this stage. She did as he bade, removing her sandals first, followed by her sundress — the material crumpling at her feet, then sat on the huge bed.

In all his naked glory, Ryan returned. He carried a dark towel in one hand which he used to rub soot and sweat from his skin, his other hand was fisted around his massive erection.

He approached the bed and, dropping the towel, rolled a condom into place. He reached for her and flipped her around until she was on her knees, running a hand down her spine until he had pressed her head onto the bed covers.

She inhaled sharply as he nudged his cock against her slick folds. It was all the warning she received. In one swift movement, he clutched her hips, hauled her back and rammed his cock into her.

The growl he released as her muscles clenched around the hard intrusion, thrummed through her body before he withdrew, only to slam in again, forcing her head deeper into the mattress.

A grin teased at her lips and her eyes rolled back. *Oh yes. This was exactly what she needed.*

CHAPTER FIVE

The bed shifted beneath her. The intense warmth of Ryan's body moved away. Keeping her breathing steady, Magda feigned sleep, despite hating the fact he was leaving her alone again. She was in his bed, a step up from taking him to hers. She also had a spell packet she needed to slot into his bed to complete the enchantment of the power of three and strengthen her love spell over him.

The whisper of jeans over his legs was followed by the soft padding of his feet towards her.

Magda chanted 'let me sleep don't throw me out' in her head when he came around the enormous bed towards her. She shifted, displaying her bare breasts into what she considered to be a more alluring position, and perceived the burn of his gaze upon her 'slumbering' form.

Heat washed over her when she sensed his head moving closer. He never touched her, but the hair on her nape prickled, she heard and felt the deep inhale through his nose, he breathed in her scent from the crook of her neck to her collarbone. Hopefully, her perfume would still be strong enough to influence him, to draw him to her.

Goose pimples erupted over her skin under the featherlight brush of his fingers across her upper arm, to the swell of her breast, and down to skim her clit before withdrawing his hand. Did she 'wake' and coax him back to bed, or stay 'asleep' so he would leave her alone in his room?

She hadn't expected this to be so easy, but she gave thanks to the universe that Ryan lived in a studio apartment above his workplace.

His tread faded, then vanished with the quiet click of the door closing behind him.

Magda held her breath for the count of three, then exhaled slowly. Repeating the exercise twice more, she was centred by the power of three. She sat up and looked around the room, taking in as many details as she could. A denim pant cuff and the dirty toe of a sock hung over the edge of the wicker hamper tucked next to a door, which stood ajar and led, if she was not mistaken, to an adjoining bathroom. An untidy stack of glossy magazines displaying cars, the butt of a gun and a forge, on top of the hamper offered an insight into his interests, and was surprised she didn't spot a dirty mag in the second pile on the bedside table.

Her bag was on the laundry basket of neatly folded clothes, her dress in a puddle on the floor next to it, shoes nestled among red roses and white cotton.

She hadn't regretted not wearing panties or a bra when she left her house, especially when it had inflamed Ryan's passion before he carried her to his apartment, but now she had nothing of hers to leave in his personal space. Gnawing on a thumb nail, she retrieved her bag. She had dropped in the miniature spray bottle of her home-made perfume, along with her cell, wallet, and the most important spell sachet. She pulled out the perfume with the packet, and spritzed herself liberally, before misting the spray around the room. Even the laundry basket was targeted while she staked her claim, scent-marking his private space.

Damp patches appeared on the bedding from the heavy concentration of perfume. She dropped the bottle and knelt on the mattress at the head of the bed, admiring the perfectly scrolled ironwork of the headboard, delicate leaves and vines fashioned into the frame. It was beautiful and, hearing the distant ring of the blacksmith's hammer falling, she was sure Ryan had literally made his own bed. She stuck her hand down a gap between the frame and the mattress, to find the pattern was repeated. A grin tugged at her mouth, the perfect place to hang the spell packet had presented itself to her.

I will have Ryan Jones as my own alpha bear.

I will have Ryan Jones as my own alpha bear.

I will have Ryan Jones as my own alpha bear.

Once the little pouch was hanging discretely on a leaf behind the head of the mattress, she scrambled off the bed, snagging her perfume on the way.

A longing glance at the bathroom was dismissed. While Magda craved a shower, it was necessary to keep Ryan's scent on her for as long as possible, even mingled with her carefully crafted fragrance, she would smell like him. It would be a smack in the olfactory senses of the bigoted old bear when she left Torben Smithworks, emphasising that the alpha did indeed have time for her, a lowly, soul-deprived human.

Ryan's scent on her when she left, would also stoke his inner beast's ego, she was sure.

Before replacing the little bottle in her bag, she gave the room one more spray. She shrugged into her dress and slid her feet into her sandals. Fingering her hair into some semblance of sexy bedhead, she swung her bag over her shoulder, and opened the door.

The clanging of the forge was amplified, the rhythmic thunk attesting to the alpha's dedication to his craft.

Magda followed the sounds of industry to the foundry floor.

Halfway down the spiral staircase, she caught sight of him. Ryan was a wonder to behold while he swung the hammer against red-hot metal, well-defined muscles dancing under his skin. She watched him until he had finished beating the glowing metal into shape, then bounced down the steps, her sandals clinking on the decorative iron.

He looked up, his gaze raking over her before he plunged his work into the water vat. The déjà vu of him disappearing into the billowing of steam was broken when he strode out of it towards her.

She stopped on the fifth step, eye level with the brooding male in front of her.

Leisurely, and with a hint of arrogance, he breathed her in, his chest heaving. She saw the gleam of amber flash across his eyes as his inner bear made his presence known. The corner of his mouth twitched, and Magda was confident he was savouring the scent of their lovemaking on her body.

"So, the forge is the mistress who keeps pulling you away from me?" she asked, a teasing smile playing across her face. She reached out one finger to capture a bead of sweat off his brow, bringing it to her mouth. His eyes widened, the amber intensified as, with deliberation, she licked the droplet off her finger.

Ryan growled, his words like a storm rolling in from the north. "I'm working to a strict deadline. It's the only thing keeping me from teaching you your place right now."

Magda cupped his jaw and lent forward to place a chaste kiss on his lips. "Say no more, my alpha. I will get out of your fur," she winked, "and let you work. I will see you at Muldoon's tomorrow night."

She walked down the last few steps, ducking under his arm resting on the corner of the railing. Without looking back, she grinned to herself when he responded.

"Tomorrow night?"

Schooling her features, she flicked her hair over her shoulder and glanced at him. "You have a deadline to meet."

She saw him frown and shake his head before she headed to the exit. She had lifted the beam and opened the door before he could gather his thoughts.

She was walking a delicate boundary, pushing against his dominant tendencies. She could lose him, but hoped for the opposite, that he would want to exert his alpha position over her the way he already had... in the bedroom.

The grouchy old man was seated at the reception desk when she made her way out of the showroom. Rather than avoid the prejudiced coot, she sidled close enough for his enhanced shifter sense of smell to pick up his alpha all over her body.

"Ryan has a deadline, he doesn't need to be disturbed by the likes of you. Make sure to keep all distractions away."

She spun on her heel, and sashayed across the floor to the door, throwing in an extra sway of her hips for good measure. He was still spluttering when the automatic doors swished closed behind her.

CHAPTER SIX

SOME MONTHS LATER - APPROACHING THE HARVEST MOON

The weight of the tiger's eye against her breastbone was comforting. It's twin, the other half of the gem was fastened to her wrist. She had searched for over a month, going through at least a quarter ton of raw rock to find one that had the right feel. Eventually, she had found a piece that held the ideal energy; shaped almost like a heart, it was perfect for splitting in two. Having it polished so it would still fit together had been tricky. The easiest part of the task was finding a jeweller able to create the setting which allowed the polished gems to be hung from the leather cords she had braided. Once completed, she kept the stones until they had charged under two full moons before she was ready to gift Ryan's to him.

Tonight was the night.

Her stomach knotted in anticipation while she walked to the bar, absorbing the increasing lunar strength of the waxing gibbous moon.

Muldoon's had become their regular haunt since Magda first met Ryan Smith. It allowed them the best of both worlds, a place to meet every night, without the prejudice of the shifters from the Torben tribe polluting the spell she was weaving around her alpha bear.

The chemistry between them was acute when they left the bar, high on red wine and caraway seeds. Some nights they didn't make it to her home before Ryan needed to sink into her. They had become well-versed in the best spots in the woods adjacent to the bar where their privacy was guaranteed.

Of course, it suited Magda to be connected to the land while they made love. It heightened the power of her spells, her affinity to the earth feeding the intention of her desire. Ryan had not looked at another woman since she had set about claiming him but, he hadn't claimed her either. If Magda wanted to keep him permanently, she needed him to bite her, seal the deal, mark her, and make her his mate. Being imbued with his power, becoming a bear shifter herself was simply a perk of being with an alpha.

Hopefully the tiger's eye would be the perfect gift. Tomorrow was the harvest moon, a powerful full moon that would supercharge the twin stones. Magda had planned to have Ryan in the clearing behind her house while the moon rose. Their bodies would join, the stones in connection while bathed in the harvest-energised lunar rays. It would be perfect. He would finally claim her, she was certain.

Ryan Jones will be mine.

Ryan Jones will be mine.

Ryan Jones wi—

Magda's mantra stuttered to a halt in her head when she rounded the corner of the street leading to Muldoon's.

Ryan was unmistakable. His towering height, broad shoulders, and bulging muscles. He was damn near a bear in his human skin as much as he was when shifted.

Her spell packets, chanted mantras, the carefully crafted salves she had massaged into his skin, her beautifully balanced perfume... everything was unravelling in front of her.

Muldoon's had six little cabins that provided accommodation for travellers. While the majority of residents who used the place were shifters, occasionally, Muldoon served humans. He was one of the few shifters who did but not unexpected given his mate was born human.

Ryan stood at the bottom of the steps in front of the premium cabin, his arms around the waist of a petite woman whose blonde hair was pulled into a messy ponytail. Their foreheads were touching, as though they were murmuring sweet nothings.

Wrath filled Magda. She had no idea who the other woman was, but she was spoiling every one of Magda's plans. *Ryan was hers*! How dare the little slut steal him from her.

Blood oozed into Magda's mouth, the metallic flavour breaking through the haze of rage. Unlocking her jaw, she released her lip. The sting was cathartic as she watched Ryan give the other woman a gentle kiss, then walk away, leaving the stranger alone on the porch, arms hugged around her scantily clad body. When Ryan disappeared into the bar, the other woman entered her cabin and shut the door.

Magda drew in a deep breath. Held it for the count of three and exhaled slowly. Two more and she was calmer... marginally.

A rational, shrewd approach to this problem was essential. Ryan was hers. It was merely a matter of reminding him how important she was.

Three more deep breaths to the count of three brought her rage under control. The weight of the tiger's eye at her wrist and against her chest centred her. She had to renew her claim on Ryan first. Flood his nose with her perfume, *her* scent not that of the other woman. She had remade the spell sachets in her bag only that morning, ready to exchange them with the ones she had placed around Ryan last month.

The sting in her mouth, the taste of blood pulled at her mind.

Blood.

Blood held power. So far, she had relied on herbal lore, her own charms, and the occasional use of a quartz crystal. She had never used blood magic but, apparently, her herbal witchcraft was not enough.

Magda thumbed the inside of her lip, the scarlet smear over the pad when she looked down, gleamed in the moonlight.

Walking to the edge of the woods, Magda knelt on the damp ground. She pressed both hands into the dirt, allowing the soft grains of soil to roll over her fingertips. With every fibre of her being, with every strand of energy she could summon from the earth, from the moon, she closed her eyes and chanted her intention to the universe.

Ryan Jones will be mine. He is mine.

Ryan Jones will be mine. He is mine.

Ryan Jones will be mine. He is mine.

Opening her eyes, she retrieved the three spell packets from her bag, she gnawed her lip to reopen the sliced skin inside her mouth. The blood pooled under her tongue and, pursing her lips, she allowed it to spill out. Three bright red drops splashed against the first packet while Magda repeated the chant.

The second and third spell packets were augmented with her blood.

They lay on the dirt, in a shaft of moonlight while she dug out her perfume. Three squirts to the hollow at the base of her throat. Three squirts to her right wrist. Three squirts to the left wrist.

Concentrating, she touched each spell packet three times before tucking them and the bottle safely in her bag. Slowly, her eyes closed, she counted to three, her fingers clutched the earth.

Centred, she stood up, brushed the dirt from her knees and strode in the direction of the bar.

Her eyes narrowed with hate when she skirted the cabin where *that* woman was staying, spotting a shadow of movement behind the blinds. The woman could wait. Magda would deal with her after she had restored her claim on Ryan.

Ryan's big black truck was parked behind Muldoon's, the door unlocked, as was his habit. The arrogance of the alpha, no one would dare to steal from the bear who would beat them to a pulp. Opening the driver's door, Magda fished between the seat and back rest, finding the sachet she had left there, and replaced it with her new, blood enhanced, spell packet. His leather jacket lay on the passenger seat, so she replaced that packet too.

When she shut the door, she caught sight of her reflection. Blood trailed down her chin. Magda stared at herself for several long seconds. The blood was stark against her pale skin. Despite the fact it heightened her lust for Ryan, seeing it on her face, lending her a wildness that was essentially Ryan, she wiped it away with the corner of her black sleeve.

She could use blood play with Ryan once she had secured her claim on him.

Satisfied she was presentable, she schooled her features, and entered the bar. Ryan would only see her love, her excitement at his presence. She couldn't let him witness her anger. Not yet.

He didn't notice her approach, too busy talking to the bear-shifter behind the bar.

"How long will your great-niece be staying?"

Magda paused. *Was Ryan talking about the slut he had been with?*

Muldoon joined the woman Ryan was talking to, draping one arm around his mate's shoulders.

"Lizzie hadn't given us any indication of her plans. She has to be back at university next week though."

"What's she studying?"

Gritting her teeth, Magda needed to stop the conversation, to insinuate herself into Ryan's mind.

"Hey there, my alpha," she cooed. Looping her arms around his neck she pressed herself against his back.

She heard him inhale her scent, tracked his reflection in the bar's mirror, his eyes glazed over, and the amber of his bear flashed across his irises.

"I have a present for you, my love."

"Yeah? What have you got?" He turned on his stool, to gather her up until she was on his lap, his arousal evident.

Concentrating on the pleasure building from their melded bodies, Magda smiled seductively. "Why don't you take me home and find out?"

Beer ignored, Ryan stood and, tucking Magda into his side, ushered her through the bar without a backward look.

When they reached the door, Magda glanced over her shoulder to see Muldoon's disapproving frown, and his mate biting her fist. With a sly grin, Magda slid a hand along the arm anchored around her body. She'd have him once more, make him forget that there had been any other woman before her, and would never be another woman again.

Ryan opened the passenger door for Magda, lifted her in and, dropping a kiss to her mouth, snapped her seat belt in place. He shut the door with a soft click, then jogged around the vehicle to open his door and climb in.

Magda waited. Watched the flex of his arm when he shifted gears and manoeuvred the car out of the parking lot towards the forge. Once away from the busiest area of town, Magda reached across the centre console to rest a hand on Ryan's leg and walked her fingers up the taut muscle of his thigh until she reached the zip of his jeans.

His breath hitched, a low rumble of approval emanated from his chest, she opened his pants and allowed his erection to spring free.

Angling her body, she ducked her head to brush the tip of his cock against her nose. She caught the whiff of another woman's juices tainting his skin. Her teeth ground together, she quashed her anger, refusing to acknowledge she knew.

She needed to re-weave her spell, assert her claim on Ryan.

Swallowing her pride, Magda opened her mouth. She let her saliva coat his cock and worked her throat, teasing the tip while her tongue flattened along the thick, pulsing vein of his dick.

He would forget every woman but her.

CHAPTER SEVEN

Anger burned in her heart. Her jaw ached from clenching her teeth. Magda shifted on the bed, Ryan's arm was slung across her hip, but he was deep in slumber, unaware of her movement. It was a win for her, to have him drop his guard sufficiently to sleep in his own bed with her.

Arching her hips, Magda made the space necessary to roll out from under Ryan. He had turned out to be a big snugly teddy bear on the nights she laced his wine heavily with caraway seeds. Of course, the drive and passion he subjected her to before he slept was always worth it.

Her enjoyment tonight had been marred because, earlier, he had been in the arms of another woman. *Had they been entangled in the same throes of passion?*

Ryan rolled over, his face on the mattress muffling the loud, gravelly snores which followed a night of overindulgence.

Confident he was dead to the world, Magda climbed off his bed to pad quietly, and without hesitation to where she had left her bag on the chair near the bathroom door. She belonged here. In Ryan's life, in his home, in his bed.

Reaching into her bag, she withdrew only the spell sachet, forgoing the usual ritual of spritzing her scent around the room. She didn't want him to stir, ready for round four.

Back on the bed, Magda replaced the bag hanging on the headboard. With the old one in her hand, she studied her bear. Her rage softened while she watched him sleep, tempted to snuggle into his arms.

He rolled over, muttering in his sleep. "Izzy."

Magda held her breath, concentrating on his nonsense, heard nothing more than *her* name before he took a snorting snore and fell silent.

The other woman had to go.

If Magda wanted to keep her bear, she needed to remove everything that diverted Ryan's attention from *Izzy*, her lip curled into a sneer at the name. Realistic in the knowledge they couldn't be together 24-7, Magda had to make her claim clear. Ryan was hers!

Resolved, she dressed quickly then snuck out the bedroom and down the stairs. Despite the workroom being quiet, the forge was still hot, bathing the space in a warmth that blocked the chill of the encroaching winter.

Ignoring the double doors into the showroom, Magda left via the private door at the back of the building. Ryan had shown it to her the first time he brought her home from

Muldoon's for the night. It bypassed the security of the shop front and allowed her to leave soundlessly.

The drive in Ryan's truck from Torben Smithworks to the border of shifter territory, gave Magda an opportunity to think about why, after months of ignoring all other females to devote his attention to Magda, would he suddenly show interest in another woman.

Even though, at this time of night there were no other vehicles about, Magda found herself rolling to a stop at the give way sign at the junction of the main road through shifter territory. Trees lined the route, spreading out for miles into the forest, yet it was the almost full moon that held her focus. It beamed down on her, framed between the avenue of trees leading to the Torben pack's township.

During the last couple of months, Magda had witnessed Ryan's growing aggression when the full moon neared. It was as if his bear prowled just below the surface. Previously, Ryan's bear had accepted Magda's place in his life without complaint. Tonight, while Ryan drank more and more of her love potion, his eyes dulled, and the bear receded. The bear was breaching her spells and, tomorrow, under the potent glow of the celestial orb, he would be dominant. It was why she had chosen the power of the harvest moon to reap the rewards of her efforts, her time spent cultivating her relationship with Ryan... by mating him.

Mating him.

Shaking her head, Magda continued towards Muldoon's. The only thing that could ruin her chances of becoming Ryan's mate was the arrival of a true mate. The thought set her teeth on edge. Ryan was hers, chosen by *her* to be the perfect mate. To revel in his prowess as a lover, to share in his power. This other woman needed to be gone before she destroyed every little thread Magda had carefully built between her and Ryan.

Muldoon's stood dark and silent against the night sky when Magda reached her destination. She drove straight to the cabin where she had seen Ryan earlier. Slamming the car into park, she turned off the ignition and removed the keys. She needed to be careful, to be cunning in the way she removed her rival from town. Ryan wasn't just an attractive male, he was addictive. His skill in the bedroom, at wringing out every last shred of pleasure possible would have the other woman eager to stay.

Fear.

Fear was a stronger motivator than passion. She had to frighten away this woman.

With a sharp nod, Magda jumped out of the truck and shut the door before jogging over to the cabin. She scanned the area, ensuring no one was around before she banged the palm of her hand against the door, taking another look around, she rapped again. Magda never let up, even when a light flickered to life the other side of the thin curtain and sound of soft footfalls approached the door. She had her hand raised ready to repeat her barrage when the door cracked open.

A sleep-filled voice croaked through the gap. "Ryan?"

Magda fisted her hand around the car keys, the bite of pain holding her anger in check. "No. I'm a friend, you aren't safe. I need to get you away from here."

"What?"

Magda tried to push the door open only to meet resistance on the other side. "Please, let me in. It's too dangerous to explain like this." She choked out the words through a trembling whisper. The woman would believe her one way or another.

The door opened, allowing Magda to see her rival for the first time up close. Stormy grey eyes regarded her through thick, sooty lashes, clear skin like porcelain. It made Magda's hand itch with the need to scratch at the flawless beauty in front of her.

The young woman wrapped her arms around her narrow waist, a shiver visibly chased across her bare arms. "What do you mean, I'm not safe?"

With a final check outside, Magda closed the door, the keys jangling in her shaking hand. "Are you alone?" she entreated, barely looking at the other woman, tweaking the curtain just enough to peer into the darkness.

"Y...y...yes."

"Good. How much do you need to pack?" Magda didn't wait for an answer. Dropping the curtain to move into the room, she hefted the open rucksack off the floor and dropped it onto the rumpled bed.

The other woman stepped in front of Magda, preventing her from opening the top drawer of the dresser. "Stop it. Tell me now, what are you playing at!"

"You, poor fool," murmured Magda. She slid her hand across the petal soft skin of the other woman's cheek. Her fingers pressed a little too tightly, but she didn't relax the pressure. "He has you believing he loves you, doesn't he?"

The blonde shoved Magda's hand away and stepped back into the dresser. "Who?"

Magda snorted softly and shook her head. "The alpha. Once a year the tribe celebrates the harvest hunt. A young, usually pretty, human woman is selected by the alpha. He sweeps her off her feet, makes her believe she is the one and only woman he will ever need. He sleeps with her, imprinting his scent on her before he takes her out into the forest promising romance." Magda turned away, lifting a hand to her mouth as though trying to choke back a sob.

The tension in the room was thick, and she had seen the wide-eyed disbelief painted across that disgustingly perfect face. Ryan had indeed wooed this woman, probably promised her the world. But he wasn't free to give himself to anyone save Magda. She had sunk her claws into him and was determined to claim him completely for herself. She had devoted too much of her time, her intention into making him hers to let him walk away now. The only one walking would be this fresh-faced little slut trying to steal Magda's desired bear from her.

A soft hand touched Magda's shoulder. "What aren't you telling me? What's the harvest hunt?"

Magda sucked in a deep, shuddering breath before she turned her head, looking at the other woman standing behind her. "Hell on earth for whichever poor, unfortunate, soul gets chosen."

"Wha... why?"

Magda shook her head, she moved away, hugging herself. "You should just trust me. It's too painful."

"You can't come in here and expect me to leave because you tell me to, so there's a harvest hunt what does that have to do with me?" the younger woman objected.

Magda spun around, letting crocodile tears fall from her eyes. Hunching forward she flexed her fingers against where she was holding her body. "It's you. You are the chosen sacrifice for the harvest hunt."

"But...but Ryan—" whispered the other woman, a hand lifting to the base of her throat, a frown marring her unblemished forehead.

Taking a step forward, Magda fixed her gaze on her captivated audience, straightened up, and made a show of steeling her spine. "He will take you so deep into the woods, you won't have any idea where you are. Then, he will slip away, leaving you alone before dark. That's when the hunt begins. First the young males, then the older ones. They stagger the time they start their hunt. If more than one finds you at the same time, they fight over you."

The blonde's hand flew to her mouth, she hissed, "What? Why?"

"For the right to rut. They will hunt you down and fuck you, whether you want them to or not. It is a sport to them, to find the alpha's prize, to lay down their scent and leave her for the next beast to find. You'll run, you'll scream, and they'll become more crazed with the desire to enjoy their sick and twisted game.

"If you're lucky, you'll find your way back to the human lands before the alpha finds you. Because when he does, his animal will be so enraged at the stench of other males on you, he will take you with such force in his craving to imprint his own smell on you once more, you'll be lucky to make it out alive." Magda's head dropped, she looked at her hands twisting together, and stepped away from her target. "Although it messed up my sister so badly, she took her own life. She couldn't live with the shame, or the pain."

"Oh... I'm sor—"

Magda rounded on her, tears burning her eyes. "Don't give me your sympathy. Just pack your damned bags and get out of here before you end up another sacrifice to the depravities of the Torben tribe."

Big fat tears dripped down the white-washed cheeks of the blonde, she turned away to open the drawers with trembling hands.

CHAPTER EIGHT

The horizon glowed with the promise of the moon rise. The lunar energy was already heavy in the air, filling Magda with barely contained anticipation. The heady aroma of her garden was empowering. She slid her fingers through the tiny yellow flower heads of the goldenrod. The petals were starting to curl closed for the night, but a few remained open to her touch.

She glanced over at the cedar tree at the edge of her garden, its branches, stripped of all but a smattering of hardy leaves, silhouetted by the burnt orange of the rapidly rising moon. It was almost time. A smile tugged at her lips; Ryan was hers. He would always be hers.

After ensuring sure that *blonde* had left town, she had returned to Ryan who stirred when she slipped back into his bed. Magda had rubbed against him, warming her chilled skin on his furnace-like body, imprinting herself on him once more, she'd taken him within her again.

That had been hours ago, a whole day where she'd been by his side constantly, distracting him with her body every time he made some comment about heading out. Magda had to keep him close; she needed him to claim her under the full harvest moon, cement their relationship with a mating bond. It took little effort to persuade him to come to her place. The promise of something special had captured his interest.

It always did. She would bombard his senses with so much pleasure he'd be dizzy with her attention and always craving more.

The kitchen door slid open. Magda spun on her heel, her smile growing when she caught Ryan's eye as he filled the brightly lit space of the doorway.

"So, here you are, witch." His words reverberated on the still air, sinking into her body.

"Here I am, Alpha," she purred.

"You promised me something special." Ryan's eyes gleamed, the light of the moon speared out from just above the trees, highlighting his face and every muscular curve of his naked body.

Magda beckoned him with the curl of a finger. Sliding her robe from her shoulders, she allowed the silk to slip to the ground and walked through her garden. The sensual caress of the leaves, flowers and seed heads heightened her senses.

Ryan let out a rumbling noise as he followed her, his heavy steps vibrating through the ground.

Turning her head, she made eye contact, winked and, walking a little faster, wound her way along the meandering pathways. Splashing through the little creek, she gasped, the chilled water reaching as high as her knees at the deepest point.

"Where are you going, woman?"

Magda laughed. "Catch me if you can, alpha." She scrambled up the opposite bank. She began to run when Ryan entered the water behind her. Earlier, she had laid out the blanket, pinned it with crystals, and lit the area with candles. Magda had been careful to use hurricane jars to make them safe in the woodland behind her home, sinking the heavy bottoms of the glassware deep into the damp soil to hold them steady.

The moon cleared above the trees; its warm orange luminescence pierced the clearing as Magda entering her meticulously crafted glade.

Large hands clamped around her hips, and Ryan swung her off the ground in a blatant demonstration of his strength. She squealed; breath caught in her throat, then giggled.

She gazed down at the dark, brooding face of the man she desired the most. "Do you plan to eat me, Alpha?"

"Perhaps." He snapped his teeth together near her belly.

He lowered her, bringing her face closer to his. Her legs slid down his side, to hook around his waist, anchoring her to him.

"Will you bite me?" she murmured. Her lips brushed over his mouth, teasing him with a barely-there kiss before she pulled away.

His nose flared, eyes dilated, lip curled back over straight white teeth. His canines thickened, the points more pronounced, growing larger before her eyes.

Magda speared her fingers into his thick locks and tugged his head back. His growl pulsed through her, her clit tingled, pussy tightening. She was wet, and only getting wetter at the promise of what was to come.

Ryan strode to the blanket, dropping to his knees so quickly, Magda's hands clutched his hair. He fell forward, his arms absorbing the impact before he sunk his cock into her warm, wet folds.

Magda arched against him. Her muscles spasmed around his hardness, her body stretching to accommodate his thickness. Her head dropped back, mouth open on a breathless moan, as he thrust into her again. Her fingers flexed against his shoulder, her nails scrapping against his taut skin. "Yessssss."

His nose nuzzled along her neck to the soft shell of her ear. The fingers of one hand dug into her waist holding her in place against him, while he thrust into her. His other hand was resting on her throat. The tiger's eye around her neck had moved, connecting with the other half of the stone that she had fastened around Ryan's wrist last night.

Magda tugged at the locks curling at his nape. His mouth opened against her neck his teeth scraped against her skin. "Take me, Alpha. I'm yours, you know this is what you want, what you need."

Pain pierced her shoulder, his teeth sinking into the muscle, blood slipping over her skin, his cock thrusting deep into her pussy, her cum sliding over them both.

Her orgasm crashed through her. Stars exploded behind her eyes. Her voice became hoarse, her scream echoed around the glade. She had never experienced anything so intense before.

Ryan pulled his teeth from her shoulder, threw his head back and roared. His cock grew larger, tighter then, his own orgasm exploded within her. Hot, thick spurts of cum hit her cervix, throwing her into another orgasm.

Heat suffused her, like fire licking at her mind. Magda thrashed her head, her skin crawled.

"You need to shift." Ryan murmured in her ear, one hand smoothing her hair back from her sweat drenched forehead. "Let your bear out, little mate. Embrace the shift." He moved away.

Panic filled her, breath struggling to come to her lungs, the pressure of... something pushing out from her centre. She rolled onto all fours, eyes wild, she searched for Ryan, locking eyes with his bear. The giant kodiak lay with his head in his paws, belly flat on the ground, stretched out like a rug.

"Ry...ry...an?" Magda panted.

The bear whined, nudging her hand with his huge wet nose.

She panted, tried to count to three, find her centre. Chaos rippled through her mind. Pain tore through her body.

Magda exploded. Her bones shattered. Skin disintegrated. Her world went black.

'*Open your eyes, little mate.*' A deep voice resonated through the atmosphere.

Magda shuddered.

'*You didn't explode, silly female. You shifted.*' The voice rubbed against her mind, prickling in the fathomless recesses of her soul.

She stayed surrounded by darkness.

'*I said open your eyes.*' The words roared in her head.

Everything hurt, like she'd been stung by a million bees. Light flickered. A blur of brown loomed in front of her.

Her sense of disembodiment faded; realisation smacked her in the face. She was slowly opening and closing her eyes. She focused on controlling her body, forced her lids to open. Her vision became sharper, the brown blob came in to focus.

Ryan's bear.

He sat back on his haunches. Nowhere near as large as he once was.

Magda trembled, commanding her body to move until she sat up. Taller than before. Stunned, Magda looked down at her hands.

She was a bear.

ABOUT LILLY RAYMAN

British born, now Australian, Lilly Rayman writes steamy paranormal romance and hot historical fantasy for Leilani Indie Publishing. In 2014, she won iParchment's best work and most popular work for An Unexpected Bonding. As a wife, mother, and farmer, when she's not writing she's reading or cooking delicious meals from scratch; her kitchen always smells of fresh bread or pizza.

To find out more and receive reader exclusives, subscribe to Lilly Rayman's newsletter today!

Follow Lilly today on social media:

bookbub.com/authors/lilly-rayman

facebook.com/lillyrayman0007

goodreads.com/lillyrayman0007

instagram.com/lilly-rayman

twitter.com/lillyrayman0007

Website

https://www.leilaniindiepublishing.com/lilly-rayman

Also by Lilly Rayman

Please visit your favourite store to discover other books by
Lilly Rayman

An Unexpected Alpha Series

An Unexpected Mating: Prequel — Out Now

An Unexpected Bonding: Book One — Out Now

An Unexpected Revelation: Book Two — Out Now

An Unexpected Hellhound: Book Three — Out Now

An Unexpected Collection: Complete Collection of
Unexpected Novellas — Out Now

Other works

A Reluctant Roxana: An Unexpected Short Story – Published
in the Dare to Shine Anthology

Red Wolf — Out Now

Women in White: Journals Through Time — Out Now

Branded in the West — Out Now

Earth Invasion 2020 — Out Now

Biting the Veteran — Out Now

www.ingramcontent.com/pod-product-compliance
Lightning Source LLC
Chambersburg PA
CBHW070118120726
47909CB00002B/650